Carl Weber's:

Five Families of New York:

Part 5: Manhattan

Carl Weber's:

Five Families of New York:

Part 5: Manhattan

C. N. Phillips

www.urbanbooks.net

Urban Books, LLC
300 Farmingdale Road, NY-Route 109
Farmingdale, NY 11735

ISBN 13: 978-1-64556-672-4

First Mass Market Printing January 2025
First Trade Paperback Printing March 2024
Printed in the United States of America

10 9 8 7 6 5 4 3 2 1

Distributed by Kensington Publishing Corp.
Submit Orders to:
Customer Service
400 Hahn Road
Westminster, MD 21157-4627
Phone: 1-800-733-3000
Fax: 1-800-659-2436

Hey, guys! C. N. here. As you all prepare to embark on the final story in the *Five Families* saga, I'd like to take the time to tell you how grateful I am that you've come along for this ride. Strange as it may seem, I am both saddened and relieved. Sad because I have grown so attached to these characters, but relieved because now you all have a complete series to enjoy whenever you want. But I must warn you that . . . Actually, I'll let you take this last journey alone. See you at the end.

Heavy is the head that wears the crown.

—William Shakespeare, *Henry IV*

Chapter 1

Manhattan, 1978

"One day you're going to wake up and everything you thought you knew will be different."

Eighteen-year-old Caesar King heard the sound of his father's voice replaying over and over inside his head. He'd interpreted the words many different ways, but never did he think he would wake up one day and end up on the wrong side of a holding cell. From where he sat on the wall, Caesar looked past the bars and clenched his jaw at the officers walking by. Some stopped to taunt him by smiling triumphantly while others sneered his way. See, Caesar wasn't a small catch. He was a big fish. Him being in their clutches made them feel powerful, and they let it show. There was one officer who walked by the cell, however, and looked like he saw a ghost when he spotted Caesar sitting there. He looked around quickly, like someone was there watching his every move, and then was gone. Caesar didn't think too much of it. He was trying to figure out what he was going to tell his dad.

The cell had five other men who took up space on the other side of it. They were having their own conversation, but every so often one of them would glance over toward where he was sitting. Caesar paid them no mind because, as far as he was concerned, he was there alone. As he sat, he leaned forward with his elbows on his knees, thinking about what transpired that evening. His eyes went to his boots and focused on the drying blood stains on them.

"You're over here lookin' like you lost ya puppy dog. It must be ya first time here," a voice said.

It belonged to a heavyset black man who took a seat next to Caesar. The others remained engrossed in their own conversation, ignoring the two of them. Glancing down at the blood on Caesar's shoes, the man pointed at them.

"That why you in here?" he asked. When Caesar ignored him, his voice got louder. "I said, is that why you're in here?"

"What's it to you?"

"Because I want to know, that's why. No need to be hostile. Let me school you on some manners. I'm Jontae. Now it's your turn. Who are you?"

"I'm a man who's in a jail cell," Caesar responded blandly.

"Man? Ha! You don't look like nothin' but a boy to me. No older than seventeen!" Jontae noted and caused Caesar to groan.

"Eighteen," Caesar corrected him.

"Same difference."

"You obviously came over here for a reason besides getting on my fucking nerves. What do you want?"

"Here you go with this hostile shit again. But to answer your question, I don't want nothin'. I guess I'm just tired of seein' you young cats throw ya lives away behind stupid shit."

"And I guess it's okay for older people like you to do it then."

"I didn't say all that. It's stupid as hell for me to be here too. And I bet you I wouldn't be if I didn't hit that motherfuckin' bottle tonight. Asshole caught me sleepin' with his girl and pulled a knife on me. And everybody knows you don't bring a knife to a gunfight. I shot that motherfucka where he stood! I ain't kill him though. I should have, because now I'm here since he lived to tell the tale." Jontae shook his head. "Now I've told you my story. What's yours, huh? Let me guess. Based on the blood on your shoes, somebody came at you wrong, and you had to teach them a lesson. What did you do, beat him up bad?"

"I killed him," Caesar answered flatly.

Jontae looked quickly around to see if anyone was paying attention. When he was sure nobody had heard what Caesar said, he turned his attention back to him and spoke in a low tone. "Are you crazy? You can't be sayin' shit like that out loud in here! Not if you want to be innocent until proven guilty."

"Now do you really think I would tell a mother-fucka I don't know and just met if I really killed somebody? Stop talking to me." Caesar's voice was rough and serious. He just wanted the man to stop talking to him and to leave him to his thoughts. He wasn't there to make friends. He was waiting.

"That's the last time I let you be disrespectful. Now I done tried to be nice to your stupid young ass. But who the fuck do you think you're talkin' to?" Jontae stood to his feet and puffed his chest out.

Suddenly the cell got quiet, and the men on the other side looked over at them. One who had a scruffy and dirty beard tried to get Jontae's attention by shaking his head quickly, but Jontae's fiery eyes were too busy glaring at Caesar.

"I'm talking to you," Caesar told him.

"You must think I'm some sucker off the street. Well, I got a news flash for you, kid. I'm not one of them. Apologize."

"Apologize?" Caesar was truly amused. He glanced over at the men tuned in intently to the scene at hand and pointed to them. "You know the reason why those men over there haven't bothered me one time? It's because they know who I am."

"And who is that exactly?"

"Somebody whose bad side you really don't want to be on."

"Ay . . . ay! Man. Leave him alone. You really don't know who that is?" the man with the scruffy beard asked Jontae. "That's Caesar King, man!"

At the mention of his name, Jontae's demeanor instantly changed. His chest went back down, and he actually took a step away, almost in fear. It seemed as though Caesar's name spoke for itself. Jontae put his hands up as if to usher in an apology.

"My bad. I . . . I didn't know."

Caesar grunted in response, and Jontae hurried back to the other side of the cell, leaving Caesar to his thoughts. Some might have seen that exchange and wondered how a grown, full-sized man was frightened by a teenager. The answer was simple. Caesar was the son and underboss of Cassius King, New York's biggest drug kingpin, which meant he was the closest thing to untouchable. Not just because he was protected, but because he was no stranger to murder. He and the grim reaper spoke the same language fluently, and Caesar wasn't afraid to get rid of anything that stood in his way.

Caesar was sure that, by then, Cassius knew of his situation and most likely wasn't too enthralled about it. Mainly because a lot of people questioned his judgment to put someone so young in charge of anything business related, but Cassius trusted his son. And for a long time, Caesar had become a master of flying under the radar. However, that evening he'd been in the right place at the wrong time. Caesar thought he'd done a good job at keeping his grass cut low, but somehow a snake still managed to slither into his yard and make a home. The name of said snake was Gerald, a young guy from the Lower East Side. Not quite as young as Caesar, but not too much older.

Gerald was hungry, and Caesar could tell by the naps in his hair and the ratty clothes he wore that he was ready to make some money. So Caesar gave him an opportunity to make some with one of the crews he oversaw. Gerald proved his worth right away, getting off the little bit of cocaine provided to him so fast that Caesar felt it was time to up his supply. That night, the two men were meeting so Caesar could front him two kilos of New York's finest. What Caesar didn't know was that Gerald was working with the cops, who were working with the Feds the whole time. Apparently he was hungrier than Caesar thought. What was supposed to be a simple drop had turned into Caesar getting busted. It was bad, really bad. But the only thing working in his favor was that Caesar didn't have any of the drugs on him. That wasn't how he conducted business, but the cops assumed he was walking around dirty and jumped the gun. They ran down on him but not before Caesar was able to get a few kicks to Gerald's skull.

Caesar was angry at the fact that he had sullied what had been, until then, a foolproof operation. But he was even more upset at the thought of letting his old man down. He tried not to think about what Cassius would have to say to him if he ever got out of the hole. But Caesar could guess that his rank would be snatched. It was his fault that Gerald had even gotten into the fold. Caesar's problem was that, although he dabbled in illegal things, he still wanted to feed the streets and present opportunities. That way of thinking had come back to bite him where the sun didn't shine. He couldn't help but feel like his father had been right with his own way of thinking. See, Cassius wanted to bleed the streets dry and not provide too many opportunities. He wanted to keep them starving so that there would always be a place for him. He always said that in order to separate the bottom from the top, there had to be a clear line that people knew not to cross.

The sound of keys jangling followed by the cell door opening caught Caesar's attention. He glanced up and saw the officer who had acted strange earlier standing there, but he wasn't alone. Caesar's father was there as well. As he suspected, Cassius didn't look too happy.

"Caesar King, it's your lucky day. You're free to go," the officer told him.

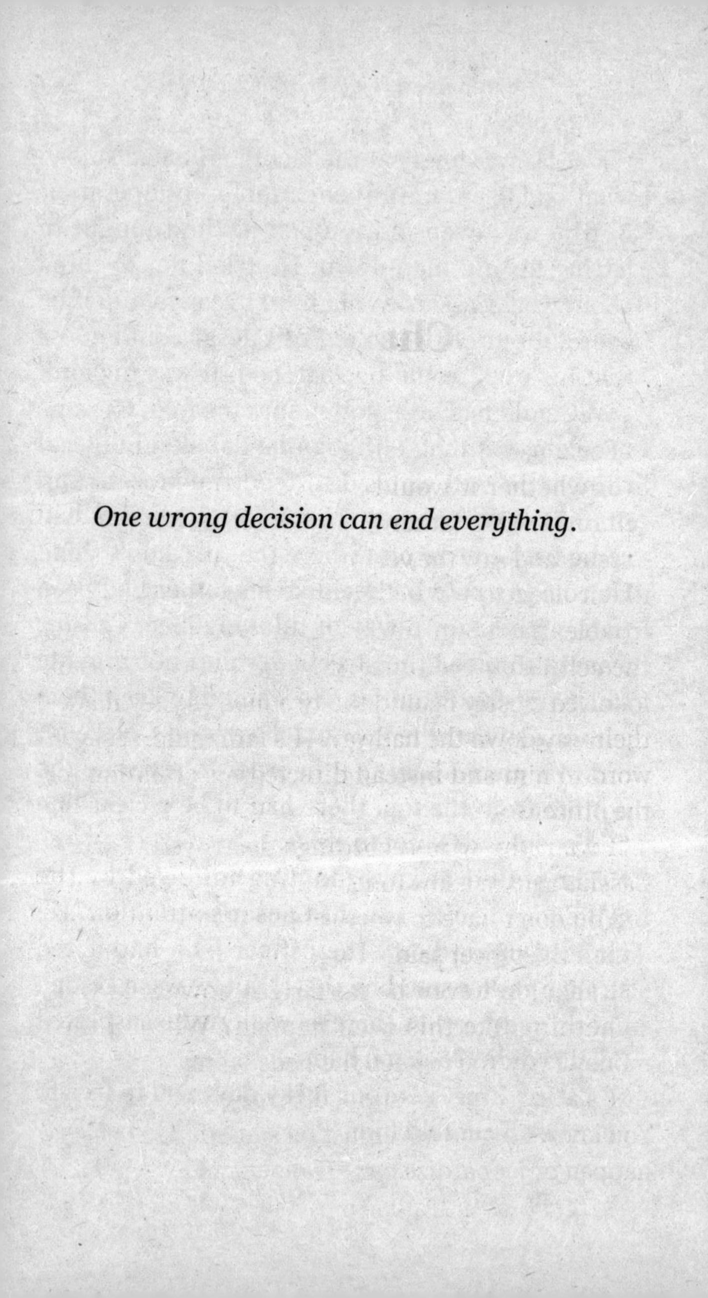

One wrong decision can end everything.

Chapter 2

For a second Caesar found himself pondering over whether it would be smarter to stay in the cell or face his father. He took one more look at Cassius and saw the vein popping out of his temple like it used to when Caesar was little and got in trouble. He got up quickly from the bench and left the cell. After the officer locked it again, Caesar followed closely behind the two men as they made their way down the hallway. His father didn't say a word to him and instead directed his attention to the officer.

"I want the wire recordings destroyed, Larry," Cassius said in a low tone.

"You don't have to worry about that. It's already done," the officer said.

"I shouldn't even be here right now. How did something like this even happen? With all the money I pay you to keep the Feds off my ass."

"I apologize. This slipped through our fingers. You know I would never just let something like this happen or jeopardize our arrangement."

"Then how did it happen?"

"That son of a bitch Gerald has been working with the Feds without us knowing. I think they know there are moles in the department, because we had no idea about any of this. That damn Detective Easley has a real hard-on for you. I don't know what he had on Gerald to make him turn rat, but he was going to use him to take you down. Lucky for you, Officer Osborne was there. He blew the bust by jumping the gun and sending a unit in before anything too incriminating was caught on the wire. He'll have some explaining to do to the captain, especially since the recordings are now missing. But don't worry about that. Like I said, it's handled, sir."

"It better be."

Caesar knew a lot about his father's business dealings, but that was the moment he really saw Cassius for the powerful man he was. Caesar had been almost positive that he would have to do some kind of time, but in just a few minutes his father's influence and money freed him.

Cassius and Caesar walked out of the precinct to an awaiting limousine parked out front. Once they drove off, Caesar waited for the lecture that he thought for sure was coming. He braced himself for his father's tongue-lashing, but it never came. In fact, Cassius didn't say a word. Instead, he just puffed on a cigar and looked out the window.

Caesar should have been relieved, but the silence was driving him crazy.

"Aren't you mad at me?" he asked, looking over at his old man.

Cassius was in the middle of taking a long, slow drag. He exhaled the smoke with his eyes shut and didn't open them again until his lungs were cleared. When he finally spoke, his gaze seemed to pierce Caesar's.

"I thought I would be. But no, I'm not mad. However, disappointed? Yes. Had you been anyone else's son, they would have tried to throw the book at you."

"I'm sorry, Dad."

"Sorry doesn't change the fact that you made what could have been the biggest mistake of your life."

"I know, but I'm still sorry."

"I know," Cassius sighed. "You let a rat in on my operation."

"I didn't think he would do something like that," Caesar said, trying to defend himself.

"Why not? You barely knew him. And he got the closest anyone has ever gotten to crushing everything I've built."

"You heard the officer. They barely got anything."

"Exactly. And that's more than anyone has ever gotten on my operation. Do you know why I'm such a successful businessman? Go ahead, ask me why."

"Why?"

"Because I know who to keep in my pocket in case something goes wrong. I also know that if I don't consider them family, they have no place at my table."

"I was just trying to give the man an opportunity. And he blew it up in my face."

"Let this be a lesson learned. I don't just welcome strays off the street, and if I do, they have to prove themselves for a long time before I let them in on the real happenings around me. I can't afford for anyone involved with me to make the kind of mistake that you made tonight. I'm not ready or willing to lose everything. I thought you were ready. Maybe I was wrong. Maybe you aren't after a—"

"I am ready!" Caesar interrupted. "I'm just . . ."

"Just what?"

"I'm still learning, Dad. I made a mistake! You want me to be, but I'm not perfect. Mama would understand that!"

Cassius's eyes grew wide on his son's last words, and the energy in the back of the limo shifted. Caesar leaned back into his seat and turned to look out the window. He was upset, and it showed all over his face. He didn't like anyone telling him what he was and wasn't. He had stumbled along the way, but that was what lessons were: hiccups that a person found a solution to. Cassius cleared his throat, and although unhappy, Caesar knew to face him.

"I don't expect you to be perfect."

"You could have fooled me."

"Maybe I spoke too soon through my own frustration," Cassius said, softening his tone. "I often forget that, although you're a lot like me, you belonged to her as well. You have her heart, the kind of heart that wants to see some kind of goodness in everyone. I'm not saying it's a bad thing. But this business has no room for that kind of heart. Because some people have no good in them but will use the goodness in you against you. It's a weakness, son, something to be reserved for only the ones you truly cherish. Do you understand?"

"Yes, sir."

"Can I trust that this won't ever happen again?"

"It won't."

"Good. Because I think it's time for a promotion."

"What?" Caesar asked, caught off guard.

"I don't want you overseeing the streets anymore. I want you by my side. Really learning the operation. Is that something you're interested in?"

"Ye . . . yeah!" Caesar's voice was enthusiastic. "Of course. You sure, Dad?"

"Positive. I think this will sharpen your decision-making skills. Plus, you're more than a knight. You're royalty in my eyes. A king. One day all of this will be yours, so it's time to start grooming you to take it over. But before then, there is one last loose end you need to tie up."

"I'm already knowing what it is. I don't like when people take my kindness for weakness."

"The first lesson in your new position: always expect them to do that. Knowing they'll do so will always put you in a position of power. Sometimes you have to kill a snake with its own venom for it to know to never mess with you."

"But it would be dead," Caesar said, making a confused face.

"Exactly."

To betray the hand that feeds you means to be one with hunger.

Chapter 3

Laughter filled the air as a small crowd stood outside of a bodega. Three of the men were known in the streets as Hoody, Avery, and Tone. They were all listening to the story of how Caesar King had fallen from grace the night before. Gerald stood in the center of them, reciting the events.

"What that Negro say to you, Big G?" Hoody was asking.

"After I told him I wanted out and to do my own thing, he told me he wasn't gon' let me buy the shit off him. So I told him I was gon' take it!"

"And then what happened?"

"Fool, look at me." Gerald stepped back and held his jacket open. "What you think happened? I cracked his skull. That's what the fuck happened. Got the product off him and got outta there."

"It looks like he cracked yours too," Hoody said, looking at the bruises and cuts on Gerald's face.

"I never said the motherfucka didn't fight back. He just wasn't a match for me. I was like a gorilla."

"Man, you're real bold to be talkin' about that shit out in the open like this. You know Cassius don't play about his work." Tone shook his head.

"I'm not worried about a Cassius or a Caesar," Gerald said, turning his nose up in a sneer. "Plus, that fool ended up gettin' bumped up later that day. He's still cookin' with the Feds as we speak. Cassius has other things to worry about, like the fall of his empire. In the meantime, y'all better get down with me before I take off. I'm about to be the king of Manhattan before you know it."

"Yeah, right! Now this man is talkin' crazy!" Hoody laughed.

"Man, fuck what these jive Negros are sayin'. I say let's get to this money!" Avery said, slapping hands with Gerald.

"A man with some sense!" Gerald said.

While he and Avery were talking, Hoody took notice of someone walking up on them. Gerald's back was turned, but Hoody nudged Tone and pointed. Their amused expressions turned serious, and Hoody tapped Gerald on the shoulder.

"What? You wanna get down with the get down now?" Gerald asked, but Hoody shook his head and pointed.

Gerald turned around and almost jumped out of his skin. He looked spooked when he saw who was walking up on him. It was Caesar, and he wasn't alone. In tow he had two big goons with him wearing long black coats, and Gerald didn't need to guess what was under them. If he hadn't peed on the side of the bodega earlier, he was sure he would have wet himself right then and there.

Caesar had a smile on his face, but that couldn't mean anything good, especially since Gerald had worked with the Feds to get him locked up. Everyone knew that was against the street code, but Gerald had gotten tired of being a lap dog for the big dog. His plan had always been to get close enough to Caesar to take him out. And since he didn't go anywhere without his muscle, Gerald knew that killing him would be out of the question. He *had* to go the other route. Caesar had been smart to not bring the kilos of cocaine with him to their meeting, but Gerald thought for sure the Feds had enough on him to hold him, especially since Gerald already knew where the kilos were. He wanted time to get them and do what needed to be done with them. Caesar always put the work in the same place: above Gerald's car tires. Gerald, of course, didn't tell the police that information because the kilos were worth $15,000 each. He planned to sell them and pocket all the money for himself. At the time it seemed smart, but now as he was staring into the set of cold eyes, he was regretting every choice he had made.

"I really enjoyed your story, especially the part about you cracking my skull," Caesar chuckled.

"Caesar, I thought you were—"

"Behind the bars that you sent me to?"

"Hold on, what?" Hoody asked, making a face. He looked from Caesar to Gerald. "Hey, explain yourself, man."

"Your friend is a rat. He set me up to be arrested," Caesar answered when Gerald seemed to have lost his voice.

"What? So all that mess you were just talkin' was what? Shit out your ass?" Tone's expression was more appalled than Hoody's.

"That's exactly what it was. He forgot one thing though. I come from a family with money long enough to pull me from the fires of hell. Speaking of which, here you go, Avery. For keeping him busy until I got here." Caesar threw Avery a small stack of money.

"No problem, boss. You know I don't fuck with no rats." Avery made a face and spit on Gerald's shoes before walking away.

"Yeah, man, I don't like that shit. Caesar, handle ya business, boss man. This is New York. There's already enough rodents runnin' around!" Tone stared at Gerald in disgust before he and Hoody followed Avery, leaving Gerald alone with Caesar.

"Get in the car, Gerald," Caesar said and walked to where a black limousine was parked on the street.

It wasn't like Gerald had much choice, because if he had, he would have booked it down the street. But the two men grabbed him by the arms before he could even think to run and forced him toward the vehicle. They threw him inside with Caesar and got in as well. The moment the door was shut, they drew their guns and pointed them at his chest.

"Check him for a wire," Caesar instructed.

"I'm not wearing one, I swear," Gerald said, putting his hands up.

"I guess I'm supposed to just take your word for it, huh? Check him."

Caesar's goons patted Gerald down and lifted his shirt to check. When they were sure he wasn't wearing a wire, they stopped manhandling him. Although he didn't have a wire on, what they didn't know was that he *was* supposed to meet with Easley later that day to give an official statement. But he didn't plan on telling Caesar that, especially with two guns pointed at him.

"Caesar, let's talk about this."

"Talk? We're past that. Did you really think you were going to get away free with what you tried to do to me?" Caesar asked.

"It wasn't me. It was that detective."

"Easley?"

"Yeah, that's the one. He caught me making a sale to some rich white kids and wanted to take me in. I didn't want to go to jail."

"So he promised you a way out if you gave him a bigger fish."

"It wasn't like that."

"That's what it's sounding and looking like to me. You should have taken the charge and done your time like a man."

"Done time for who? You? A little boy?"

"There it is," Caesar said with a slow smile. "Finally the truth comes out. You couldn't handle taking orders from somebody younger than you. I don't know why you motherfuckas act and think like that. Your egos are too big. They get in the way of business."

"The only reason you're where you are is because of your daddy."

"If you really think my father is the kind of man who just gives people anything because they want it, you're sadly mistaken. You could have worked your way up in the ranks and been set. But no. You got greedy. You stole from me."

"I don't know what you're talking about."

"Let's not play dumb here. You know exactly what I'm talking about. Where are my drugs, Gerald?"

"I don't know. You never gave them to me."

"But you know where I put them. Your car is parked down the street there." Caesar pointed. "That meant you had to move my drugs to drive it. And don't try to tell me the Feds got the kilos, because I know they didn't. So this is the last time I'll ask you nicely. Where is my shit?"

Gerald swallowed as he contemplated telling Caesar where they were. But he figured they'd just kill him and dump the body if he made it that easy for them. "I can take you to them," he finally told them.

"That's not an option."

"Then I don't know how you're going to get them."

"You're gonna tell me where they are one way or the other–willingly or forced. It doesn't make a difference to me."

"Either way you're gonna kill me."

"Mm." Caesar shrugged. "I think maybe we can work something out. I mean, I'm not behind bars anymore, and I like to think of myself as a nice guy."

His voice sounded sincere, but still Gerald didn't trust him. His eyes went again to the guns and then to his own hands. He saw that they were shaking slightly. He had never pegged himself as someone who was scared of death, but as he sat in her grip, he was very much so afraid.

"They're in the trunk of my car," Gerald said finally.

"Keys," Caesar instructed him, and Gerald dug in his pocket and gave them to him.

Caesar then handed the keys to one of his henchmen, who got out and went to Gerald's car. Sweat beads fell down the sides of Gerald's face as he waited for the man to get back. It was like he could hear his own heart pounding in his ears, but it was really just his blood rushing. When the man returned, he was holding a plastic bag. Inside were Caesar's two missing kilos. After Caesar inspected them, he nodded his head.

"Thank you for not making that too difficult," Caesar said.

Gerald almost gave a sigh of relief, but then he noticed the same henchman who had just retrieved the cocaine screwing a silencer on his gun. Gerald's eyes grew big, and he tried to pull the door handle, but it was locked.

"Hey, man. You said we could work somethin' out! I told you where your drugs were!"

"I did say we could work something out, and that's why I'm giving you a quick death instead of torturing you for days like I originally wanted to do. But you had to know there was no way I was going to let a rat like you roam my streets."

"Caesar. Come on, man! Caesar!" Gerald turned to the window of the limo and started hitting on it in hopes someone passing by would hear him through the tinted windows. "Help! Help! He's gonna k—"

Pft!

The silenced bullet caught him in the temple, instantly stopping any more words from coming out of his mouth. Before he slumped over, Caesar's other henchman grabbed a black trash bag from the side of his seat and covered his top half and laid him on his side before he could leak blood onto the seat.

Always stay only one step ahead so you can still hear what's going on behind you.

Cha[illegible]

[illegible] one of [illegible]

[illegible]

[illegible] the stairs [illegible] the second [illegible]

[illegible] in the [illegible]

There were [illegible] bedrooms [illegible]

just his office and a [illegible]

[illegible] in their [illegible]

Chapter 4

Caesar went home after the situation with Gerald was handled. He wanted to let his father know personally that it had been taken care of. His driver dropped him off in front of the family town house in Manhattan, and he instantly noticed a car parked outside that he hadn't seen before. Bounding up the steps that led to the front door, he burst inside the house, frightening the middle-aged housekeepers cleaning the foyer.

"Sorry. Where's my dad?" he asked.

"In his study," one of them answered.

"Thank you."

He stepped around them and made his way up the staircase to the second level of the home. His father's office was in the south wing of the house. There were no bedrooms in that wing of the house, just his office and a library, which was always quiet because nobody in their family read books. When company was over, they would almost always find themselves in the kitchen or at the bar.

Walking down the hallway, Caesar noticed that the office door was shut. He hesitated at first, wondering if maybe Cassius had female company. He didn't want to interrupt, but when he got up to the door, he heard two male voices. Caesar cleared his throat before his knuckles rapped the thick wood.

"Who is it?" Cassius called.

"It's me, Dad."

"Come in!"

Caesar opened the door and saw his father sitting at his desk while a white man in a suit sat across from him. He wasn't just any white man. He was the same detective who had arrested Caesar the night before. What was he doing in their home? Caesar found himself glaring at the man.

"Son, I think you know Detective Easley," Cassius said, motioning toward the detective.

"I do, but I'd be lying if I said it was a pleasure," Caesar told him.

He went to stand on his father's side of the desk to face Easley. He crossed his arms and leaned on the wall behind him. Easley eyed him down, but Caesar didn't look away or blink.

Easley smirked and turned back to Cassius. "Your son knows how to make an entrance, doesn't he?"

"What's that supposed to mean?" Caesar asked.

"He means we were just talking about you."

"Oh, yeah? What was said?"

"Just how it's mighty ironic how every piece of evidence I had against you magically disappeared." Easley directed his words at Caesar, but he stared at Cassius. "Must be some kind of pull you have there. I heard you were the one who came and got him out. No lawyer, just you. I'd say that's quite intriguing."

"I don't know what you're talking about. I simply went down and got out of jail my teenage son who was being falsely imprisoned."

"Falsely?" Easley scoffed. "I busted him myself."

"Doing what?"

"Selling drugs. I heard the whole deal go down."

"So you confiscated them? The drugs I mean."

"They weren't on the scene," Easley said through clenched teeth.

"Then he wasn't selling drugs. Maybe they were just talking in slang. You know how these kids are nowadays. It's a shame you don't have the recordings. How sad is it that you people turn folks against their own for your personal agendas. Now you don't have any evidence, and you turned my son's friend against him."

"Cut the bullshit. You and I both know Caesar and Gerald weren't friends. Gerald worked for him. And I know you had something to do with the wire recordings going missing."

"I think you need to take that up with someone at the precinct."

"That's the thing. I did. And they don't seem to know anything either. Which means they either innocently got misplaced, which I know is a load of crap, or you have a mole in the office. Maybe even a few of them."

Cassius's face didn't so much as twitch. Caesar could tell that the detective was trying to get a reaction out of his father, but he obviously didn't know who he was dealing with. Cassius grabbed a bottle of brandy from the corner of his desk and poured himself a glass without offering Easley any.

"I would have to be some sort of criminal to even want to do something like that," he said after taking a sip of the drink.

"What exactly are you, Cassius?"

"I'm a businessman. I'm sure you are privy to all the very legal business dealings I have in Manhattan, including the movie theater I just opened. Just because I have my hands in a lot of things doesn't make me a criminal, Detective. Now did you have an actual reason for showing up here today, or did you just want to see the inside of my house?"

Detective Easley looked from Cassius to Caesar and then back to Cassius. A small chuckle escaped his lips, and he stood. After placing his fedora on his head, he tipped it to them.

"I guess I'll just be going then. Oh, and Cassius, one more thing before I leave. You might want to teach your son whatever magic you know for keeping your nose clean. He's your weak link. A man will do anything to keep his son safe, even show his hand."

On that note, he turned his back on them. When he was out of the office, Cassius grabbed his desk phone and called the housekeeper's phone downstairs.

"Our guest is coming down. Make sure he doesn't make any detours on the way out," he said into the receiver and hung up.

Caesar was biting the inside of his cheek, visually angry at Easley's words. Cassius took one look at Caesar's face and laughed. Caesar didn't know what was so funny, and he didn't join in. Cassius took another sip from his glass and motioned for Caesar to take the seat Easley had just vacated.

"Are you upset because of what that detective said?" he asked his son, setting the glass back on the desk.

"He called me your weak link," Caesar grumbled, dropping down into the seat.

"He's a Fed. That's what he's supposed to say. Anything to get under my skin. But you . . . Why are you so upset at the truth?"

"You think I'm your weak link?" Caesar was slightly shocked at his father's revelation.

"Not think, know. As he said, you're my son. I'll do anything for you. Even die for you. I said that I'm not ready to lose my empire, but even still, if your life were on the line, I would give it all up. I told you that kind of compassion is reserved only for those who truly matter. And you are the one thing that truly matters to me. But because I know all of this, nobody can use it against me."

"Why not?"

"Because their biggest mistake will always be underestimating you. And that will always put me at an advantage. Anyway, did you handle that today?"

Caesar was still replaying Cassius's words in his head, trying to comprehend them correctly. He almost didn't hear the sentence. He nodded his head in response. "Yeah. That's what I was coming to tell you."

"And his body?"

"Burned like a witch at the stake. By now he's not anything but a pile of ashes. His car was smashed in the junkyard."

"Good. One less problem to worry about."

"Yeah, but I think the detective might be a new problem."

"I think so too. But we can worry about that a different time. Right now we have other things to discuss."

"What happened?" Caesar asked, recognizing the serious tone in his voice.

"One of our crews was found dead this morning in Queens. Word is they got into a spat with the Mexicans about territory. I'm taking this very personally."

"Have you ever thought about just talking with whoever runs things over that way?"

"Caesar, listen to yourself. Did you not hear me when I just told you they killed my men? Your cousin Bobby was one of them. There is no way I'm letting that kind of behavior slide."

"Then it's going to be a never-ending cycle of bloodshed. I've never understood why the boroughs are so separated instead of working together."

"It wouldn't work. It would be too much of a power struggle. The Italians hate us, the Chinese look down on us, the Dominicans think that Harlem is its own separate borough, and the Mexicans keep killing us. Working together with them when so many wars have happened and so much blood has already been spilled would be disastrous."

Caesar sighed. His father could be so wise at times, yet so stubborn at others. But he was right. Caesar couldn't think of a clear course of action where everyone could coexist peacefully.

"But we will get to retaliating against them at a later time. That must be a calculated move, something to send a message. But until then, I need you to start getting ready for tonight."

"What's tonight?" Caesar asked.

"Tonight you meet my business partner, Nasir Lucas."

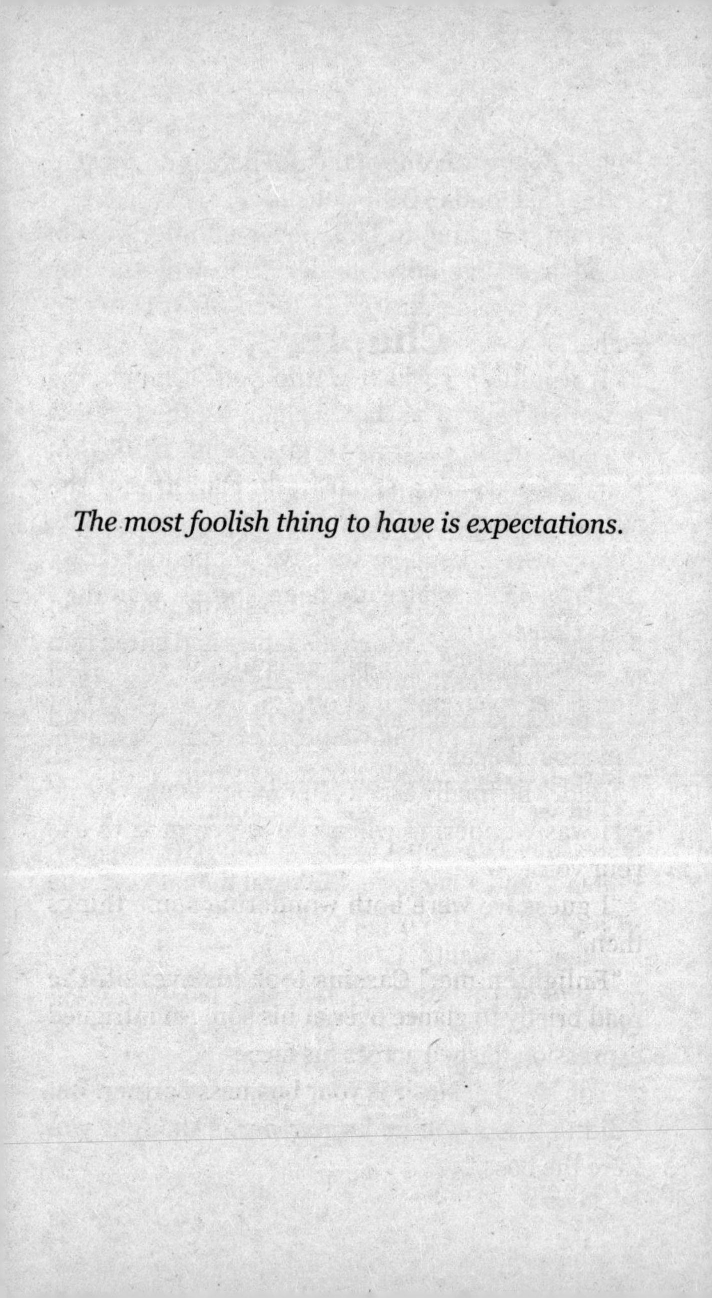

The most foolish thing to have is expectations.

Chapter 5

That night, Cassius opted to drive his own car to their destination with their goons following closely behind in another. Caesar sat in the passenger seat not saying too much but thinking quite a bit. He was dressed in his best business attire and even had put on the gold watch his father had gifted him for his eighteenth birthday. His eyes were glued to the second hand, and he watched it tick around and around again.

"Dad?" he finally asked after a long while.

"I was wondering when you were going to use your voice."

"I guess we were both wondering some things then."

"Enlighten me." Cassius took his eyes off the road briefly to glance over at his son. An intrigued expression flashed across his face.

"You say that Nasir is your business partner. But I didn't know you had a partner. I thought you were the boss."

"I am, but he is too. He's more of the silent kind though."

"How did you meet him? I've heard . . . things about him."

"And I'm sure they're all true."

Caesar paused for a moment. The streets of New York didn't say Nasir's name. They whispered it. The stories that followed weren't pleasant. In fact, they were downright terrifying. Nasir was said to be no regular man. People described him to be more of a demon. He was merciless. They said he loved business and money so much that he couldn't die. Some said his soul was attached to the game. Others said he sold it *for* the game. They were just stories to Caesar, but still he couldn't help but wonder how his father had come to get in cahoots with him.

"How did you two get into business together?"

"We're the two most powerful men in New York. Us crossing paths was inevitable. We found that we could either kill each other or work together. I think it's obvious which one we chose."

"And why do you want me to meet him now?" Caesar asked, and Cassius laughed as if he had told a joke.

"I am no fool, son. I have lived longer than most men who had the pleasure and curse of being in my position. There is only one way out for men like me, but before that time comes, I need to make sure you're ready to take over where I left off. And that includes becoming familiar with all the important players. Nasir is one of them."

Caesar nodded and grew quiet. He fell back into a sea of his own thoughts for the rest of the ride to Staten Island. It was a part of New York that he didn't frequent. The Italians didn't take too well to running into outsiders in their part of town. It made for a good place for someone like Nasir to stay off the map. When they drove through the gates of a large residence, Caesar took notice of a few armed Italian men standing guard outside the home.

"He works with the Italians, too?" Caesar asked, shocked. "I wonder how he pulled that off."

"Nasir is feared by many. He has connections in more than just New York. Come on. He's expecting us."

Cassius parked the car, and the two of them got out. Their goons did the same and followed them to the front door. The Italian men directly in their way moved to grant them entrance, but not before smirking at them. Caesar wanted to wipe the smiles from their faces. Something about them made him uneasy.

"Follow me," an Italian inside the house said.

He led them to a large office at the back of the house. Once there, he instructed Cassius's men to stand outside the room before allowing Cassius and Caesar inside, closing the door behind them. In the corners of the room were four life-sized solid gold lion statues. Each was posed differently. As Caesar looked around at the wall decor, he noticed that lions seemed to be the theme. There was even a lion hide rug in front of the desk. Sitting behind it was a skinny dark-skinned man with beady black eyes. He was much younger than Cassius and looked to be in his early thirties. His bony hands were clasped together, but he unclasped them to gesture for them to sit down.

"Nasir, it's good to see you," Cassius said once he was seated. "I appreciate you for seeing me on such short notice."

"You made it sound urgent, so I made myself available. Does it have something to do with the new shipment we just received?"

Caesar took note of how surprisingly deep Nasir's voice was. He sounded like he should have been the narrator for a black hair commercial. It was hard to keep a straight face with the thought in his mind, but Caesar managed.

"No, everything is running smoothly with that," Cassius told him. "This has to do with more sensitive matters."

"Mmm, sounds bloody."

"Possibly," Cassius said.

Nasir sighed and turned his attention to Caesar. He studied him, and Caesar didn't bat an eye. He was used to people doing that to him by then. He always figured it was because he was so young, or maybe they were just trying to test his temperature. Either way, he didn't budge. He just stared right back.

"You must be the son I've heard so much about," Nasir said, studying him. "You're not what I expected."

"That was your first mistake. You shouldn't have expected anything," Caesar responded smoothly.

"Well, if I didn't before, I know for sure now that you are the son of Cassius King. So tell me, is it true that you're as ruthless as they come?"

"I guess that just depends on what your definition of ruthless is. I'm serious about my business if that's what you're asking."

"That wasn't what I was asking. How old were you when you killed for the first time?"

"What?" Caesar was thrown off by the question. "Why is that important?"

"Because it is."

Caesar looked over at Cassius, wondering if it was a joke. But the look he received back was one urging him to answer the question. Caesar turned back to Nasir and clenched his jaw before speaking. His first kill wasn't one he liked to relive. Most people claimed to have no emotion after they killed someone, but not Caesar. He remembered the pure white rage coursing through his body when he killed the Mexican man. It wasn't too long after his mother was murdered and they were at war with all the other families, just like they still were. He didn't know which family was responsible for killing his mother, so Caesar went on a rampage on all of them.

"Fourteen," he finally answered.

"Why did you choose to become a killer so young?"

"I was angry. Someone killed my mother."

"Did you ever find out who?" Nasir asked.

"No. So everyone paid the price for it. I learned to control my emotions, but killing never bothered me. If they're meant to be on this earth, their souls will recycle."

Nasir's brows raised for a split second before they dropped and his expression went blank again. Caesar couldn't tell if he was stunned or impressed. However, the truth was the truth. The moment someone presented themselves as his enemy, it was over for them. He had gotten quite good at eliminating his foes. Gerald was the only one who almost had slipped through the cracks. But in his own defense, he hadn't known that Gerald was an enemy, or else he would have been dead a long time ago.

"Interesting," Nasir said. He turned to Cassius and nodded his approval. "If what I've heard about him is true, and what he says is fact and not fiction, I'd have to say that your son is very impressive."

"Oh, he's more than that." Cassius's voice had a proud undertone. "That's why I brought him here with me today, so he can hear what I'm about to say too. It's time."

"Time for what?" Nasir asked. Both he and Caesar gave Cassius their undivided attention.

"You know what it's time for. Expansion in our own state. I'm tired of limitations! And I know you are too. We need to make our move on every borough. Apparently you have the Italians eating out of the palm of your hand right now. We could merge business between Manhattan and Staten Island."

"As good as that sounds, you're forgetting one thing. The Italians hate us."

"I don't see how that's possible. You have the motherfuckas outside of your house right now."

"That's . . . different business. It has nothing to do with what we have going on."

"Care to enlighten me?"

"Do I ask you about your business dealings outside of you and me?" Nasir asked, and Caesar watched a glint of annoyance wash across his eyes. "If it had something to do with the drugs we move together, you would know. But it doesn't."

"Speak," Cassius demanded, and Nasir groaned.

"Fine. When I moved my black ass over this way to keep a low profile, the Italians didn't like it at first. They wanted me out of their territory, especially knowing my affiliation with you. But then I guess Benzino figured someone of my skills could be useful."

"How so?"

"He started hiring me to take care of things."

"You mean robbing people like the Tollivers in Brooklyn? Or killing motherfuckas like the Chinese?"

"I can't say. Just know the job always gets done. In return, I get to live over this way and I have more muscle for protection. You and I both know I've made more enemies than anyone in the world."

"That still doesn't explain why the Italians wouldn't become our allies."

"They hire me, not the other way around. They're greedy motherfuckas. If there is a whole pie, they want the whole pie. Not a piece of it."

"They only have a piece right now. And I would be offering them another slice. Every time business is done in another territory, a war ensues. No family can make money in another's domain, and I'm going to change that."

"And how do you plan on doing this?"

"I want to merge the boroughs. Domino seems to have forgotten that he is still in my territory.

Still, even I can't deny the power he has. I would be willing to continue to allow him to keep moving separate as long as dues are paid to me. And not just from him. The Chens, the Tollivers, and the Alverezes, too. You know they can't beat us. But I can't do it without you on board."

"You truly want to be the king of New York?"

"With you by my side of course."

"You'll have to let me think on it."

"Think on it?" Cassius exclaimed. "It's now or never."

"I just can't see a way this can work. The other families will never agree to working under you and letting you extort them."

"They won't have a choice. Either they can come the easy way, or I'll bleed them dry and just take what I want."

"Cassius, you've never fought them all at once."

"You're right. But hopefully I won't be alone. And if you get the Italians on board, there is no way we'll lose. Imagine how much money we can make by expanding in New York alone. I'm tired of losing money and product when my boys cross territory lines."

"I'll talk to them," Nasir sighed and then looked at Caesar. "Is he this pushy with you?"

"When he has his mind on something, he usually gets it." Caesar grinned.

"I guess that's something we have in common then."

"That's why we have always done such great business together. I'll be hearing from you soon?"

"Soon," Nassir confirmed, standing up.

He shook Cassius's hand before shaking Caesar's, and the men departed.

Loyalty to others sometimes can mean you aren't being true to self.

Chapter 6

"Mmmm!" A moan inevitably came from Caesar's mouth.

Inevitably because he'd been holding it in the moment Amira Rockland wrapped her full lips around the tip of his erect penis and sent him to heaven. He watched her mouth wet his entire shaft and force his manhood down her throat repeatedly. The only sound that filled the air was her sucking and slurping.

Amira was three years older than him and worked in the King family mansion as a housekeeper. Her grandmother, Pricilla, also worked there and had gotten her the job. The moment Caesar laid eyes on her, he knew he had to have her. She was a beautiful caramel brown thing and wore her thick sandy brown hair in an Afro poof at the top of her head. He liked that, especially since most of the girls were going to get their hair straightened like the white girls on TV. Not Amira, though. She stayed true to her roots.

He felt a sudden buildup and knew he was about to blow. He gripped the back of her head so that she wouldn't move and erupted into her mouth. She swallowed every drop of his cum like a champion. Caesar clenched his eyes shut and bit his bottom lip, not wanting to shout. Stars were dancing behind his eyelids, and he instantly felt his body grow tired from the powerful orgasm. He let the back of her head go, and she came up for air, wiping the corners of her mouth. She had a triumphant sparkle in her eyes as she looked down at him, and he grinned.

"You look happy with yourself," he said.

"I am whenever I please you," she told him.

She fell down on the bed next to him and nestled her head into his shoulder. He pulled his cover over them so that they could cuddle in its warm comfort. When he first saw Amira, his dick had done all the talking. He had just wanted to jump her bones and send her on her way like all the rest. Caesar wasn't a dog, but he was young. Not only that, but he wasn't in the business where he really had time to invest into a relationship. Amira, however, had changed that way of thinking. She was different, and she made him laugh. He liked having her around. In fact, most times when she snuck into his room, they didn't do anything of the sexual nature. Sometimes they just talked, and others she just listened to him vent about whatever he wanted to talk about. That night she chose on her own to let her mouth speak in other ways.

"You're amazing," Caesar said and kissed her on her forehead.

"I could just tell that you were tense, that's all. Wanna talk about it?"

"Not really."

"That's fine too," she said gently.

They lay in silence for a few moments before it began to gnaw at him. That was another thing about Amira–she had a way of getting him to talk without forcing him to. It was her safe energy. He didn't feel that he had to be so hardened with her because she accepted him for everything he was.

"Fine, you talked it out of me," he sighed, and she laughed. "It's Gerald."

"Gerald?" she asked seriously and propped herself up on her elbow.

"Yeah. That motherfucka crossed me."

"What you mean?"

"He turned out to be a fucking rat."

"Gerald?" She made a sound of disbelief. "I grew up with him. He ain't no rat."

"You try telling that to the Feds who picked me up. That man you grew up with was wearing a wire."

"Oh, my God. Caesar, are you goin' to jail? I don't want you to go to jail."

"You won't have to worry about that. Luckily for me, my father was able to get me up out of that jam."

"But didn't you just say that Gerald was wearin' a wire? My uncle got caught up behind some shit like that. He got fifty years 'cause of the recorded evidence against him. How can you get out of that?"

"Influence," was all Caesar said. "Let's just say the recordings went bye-bye."

"Good," Amira sighed in relief. "Because I don't wanna be the girl of no jailbird."

"Girl?" he asked, and she grew embarrassed.

"I'm sorry. Maybe I got ahead of myself. I just thought—"

"Right."

"What?"

"You thought right," he said and kissed her pink lips. "You're my lady."

"I'm your lady?" she said with a smile.

"You knew that already. And I don't want you cleaning this house no more either. You or your granny. I'ma get you a house somewhere nice. I don't want my woman getting her hands dirty with nothing, except maybe some shopping."

She squealed and embraced him tightly with her face against his neck. He couldn't lie. It felt good. He'd never been in a serious relationship before. But he knew Amira was like a needle in a haystack. She knew he was well-off, but she had never asked him for anything. And the things she gave him were priceless. She deserved everything he was about to give her. Especially if what his father wanted came to fruition.

Just like that he was back to reality. The smile left his lips, and he lay back on his pillow. His eyes surveyed the ceiling as if he were looking for something. Answers maybe. There was an internal battle waging a war inside him every day. Caesar knew he had done his share of adding fuel to the fire with the feuds between the other families in New York. He had been by his father's side when they set fire to one of the Chen family restaurants just for delivering on their side of town. He was also there when his father poured acid down the throat of members of the Alverez family for receiving a weapons shipment in Manhattan. But whenever something like that happened, the King family took a hit also. It was like a never-ending game of Ping-Pong that nobody would ever win. There was some good in his father's plan, but Caesar could also see the bad. Cassius didn't want to unite the families. He wanted to rule them.

"Somethin' else is on your mind, huh?" Amira asked, surveying his face.

"Nah . . . I mean, I guess. It's just my father."

"You're scared he won't accept me?"

"What? No. That's not it. It's this business deal he's trying to put together."

"What kind of business deal?"

"He wants to merge the five families. I just don't know how to feel about it right now is all."

"You think that's a bad thing? You're always talkin' about how tired you are of all the fightin' and killin'."

"It's not about what he's doing. It's about *how* he plans on doing it. If I know my father like I know I do, if they don't agree to his proposal the first time, he's going to bleed the streets dry. He's going to force them into submission. Probably make them sign over the deeds to all their businesses."

"He has the power to do that?"

"My family is the only one who has fought with every family and won every time."

"But that's one family at a time. How does he plan to beat them all at once?"

"He's found a way. And when it happens, he expects me to be at his side."

"Is that what you want?"

"He's my dad. My loyalty lies with him."

"But if you don't agree with what he's doin', then how can it? I know you're young, Caesar, but you're one of the smartest people I've ever met in my life. You don't just think things. You feel things. And my granny always tells me to always follow my gut. What is yours tellin' you?"

"That there has to be another way. I just can't think of it right now."

"Then find it. Before any more blood gets shed in these streets."

"I don't know if I have that much time. We met with my dad's business partner yesterday. They already have something cooking up."

"Business partner? I never took Mr. King for someone who worked well with others. Who is it?"

"Nasir Lucas."

At the mention of his name Amira sat up straight and looked at Caesar with wide eyes. He saw the fear written all over her face. He figured it was because of all the stories that had been spread about him.

"The Grim Reaper? You actually met him?"

"Yesterday."

"I don't know anybody who's actually met him in real life besides you and my grandmother."

"How did she know him?"

"She used to clean his parents' house before they were murdered. She told me it was his fault they died, but I don't really know the story. Now, though, he's supposed to have some sort of deep mob ties. Untouchable type shit."

"I don't know about all of that. He seemed pretty regular when I saw him."

"My grandma also always says that a great gambler never shows his hands until he knows he's won. Be careful."

"Always."

"Good." Amira kissed him again and made to get out of bed.

"Where you going?"

"I have to get a start on my daily duties. My grandma will kill me if I don't get the stairs right this time."

"Girl, didn't I just say you don't have to clean this house anymore? Matter of fact, let me make it clearer." He leaned his head back and shouted, "You're fired!" He playfully tickled her and sent her into a fit of laughter.

"I've never been fired before." She bit her lip at him.

"Well, now you know what it feels like."

"I've been making my own money since I was fifteen. I don't know what I'm gonna do with myself."

"I'm sure you'll figure it out. Especially with the monthly allowance I'm going to give you."

"Allowance?"

"Yes. Allowance. It will be more than my father was paying you to clean this big-ass house, I'm sure. Now come and show me exactly how you like to please me again."

They threw the covers over their heads and began to engage in another act of lovemaking.

Death is rarely ever the answer.

Chapter 7

After they were done making love, Caesar sent Amira and her grandmother home for the day. There were other housekeepers there who could cover their workload for them. He got dressed in a pair of blue bell bottoms and a silk button-up that he left open at the top. The cook, Martina, fixed his usual egg, bacon, and cheese breakfast sandwich for him when he got to the kitchen. She'd been cooking for them since he was younger, and she knew how he liked all of his meals. Caesar sat patiently and read the newspaper until it was finished.

"Anything good in there?"

Caesar lowered the paper in time to see his father taking a seat across from him at the table. He folded the paper and slid it to his father to take a look for himself. At that moment, the cook placed his hot sandwich down in front of him.

"Will it be orange juice or apple juice this mornin', honey?" Martina asked Caesar.

"Orange juice will be good."

"Comin' right up. Mr. King, what can I conjure up for you for breakfast?"

"How about you just make one of those sandwiches for me too? Since you already have all of the stuff for it out."

"You sure? It's really no trouble at all."

"I'm sure. If I knew how to cook a lick of anything, I would make it myself and get you off your feet," Cassius said, flapping the newspaper open.

"Mr. King, don't start this again. I am fine."

"Have you been taking your diabetes medicine?"

"Yes, I have."

"Have you been drinking enough water?"

"Yes, I have!" Martina said with an attitude and threw a hand on her hip. "Is it me taking care of you, or are you taking care of me?"

"I'd like to think of it as a little bit of give and take. You've been with us since Caesar was just a baby. I would hate for anything to happen to you."

"Well, then you know my fear every day when it comes to you. Now hush up and let me make your breakfast."

Caesar found himself smiling at the exchange. Martina was the only one who had ever been able to get away with talking to Cassius any kind of way. Probably because she had become more like family. She went on to make his food and poured them both glasses of orange juice. After she brought some grape jelly to the table, she went on to clean the kitchen.

"Did you see this?" Cassius asked, pointing at an article in the paper.

"I just skimmed through it. What's it say, Dad?"

"Looks like the Mexicans have gotten themselves into a world of trouble. The police found over a hundred guns and explosives in one of Damián Alverez's warehouses. Five arrests were made."

"Was Damián one of them?"

"No. I recognize two of these names though. Sergio and Aarón Alverez are his cousins."

"Still, I would hate to be Damián right now." Caesar shook his head.

"This is perfect. You know what this means, right? It's going to be easy to get Damián to fall in line right now."

"I'm sure his cousins are going to take the fall and not talk."

"If they follow the same code as we do in our camp, I'm sure they won't talk either. Still, the Feds are going to be watching Damián mighty close, and if he's smart, he's not going to want any more fire under his ass. Fighting me will be the last thing he wants to try, especially since the Italians have agreed to assist in my takeover."

"That was quick," Caesar said in a surprised manner.

"Nasir can be very convincing when I need him to be. Once we have the Alverez family where we want them to be, the Chens will be next. Then the

Tollivers won't have a choice but to follow suit. As far as the Dominicans, as I said before, I've allowed them to conduct business in peace for long enough. They'll do whatever I need them to. New times are amid New York, and what a magnificent sight it will be."

Caesar could tell by his father's tone that he was excited. He wished like hell that he could join in on the excitement, but he couldn't. Nothing about it seemed right. It would be different if the other territories were just up for grabs, but they weren't. The other families had done exactly what the Kings had done for years—built their empires. And Caesar knew how he would feel if someone tried to come and take it for themselves. It would be like losing freedom. He'd done a lot of things for Cassius that he never questioned. But that? It didn't resonate with him at all. If loyalty to his father meant doing something he didn't agree with, how would he ever become his own man?

"Dad?" Caesar found himself speaking before he had completely formulated what he wanted to say.

"Hmm?" Cassius asked, looking down at his plate.

"Are you sure there isn't another way to get what you want? I mean, this seems a little drastic. I'm sure if you talk to the other families—"

"Talk?"

"Yes. As in sit down and have a civilized conversation. Because for as long as I can think back to,

I remember a lot of things happening. Fighting. Killing. Plotting. More killing. But never a simple conversation."

"And do you know why that is? Too much blood has been spilled on all sides. That's nothing a simple conversation can fix. It's time for me to go all in and take what's mine."

"Yours?"

"Yes, mine." Cassius paused, spreading jelly on his bread. "I'm going to make Pangea whole again. No point in being a kingpin if I can't be the king of it all. And once I have all the power, then I'll go for Staten Island, too. Some might disagree, but for me, a good game of chess consists of every piece falling to one king. Me."

There it was, the dictator in him rearing its face. Moments like the one Cassius had just shared with Martina sometimes made Caesar forget the kind of man he was. Power fueled him. And he wouldn't stop until he felt he had it all. He liked to have everyone in the palm of his hand. That way he could crush them whenever he felt like it.

When Caesar first started on the same path his father was on, he wanted to be just like him, especially after his mother was killed. He wanted to be strong and feared, just like Cassius. But even at that age he knew he was sending himself on a path of self-destruction. He would always be a soldier no matter his rank in the game, but control was where true power lay. Control led to a certain level of consciousness that Caesar was destined to reach. He still wanted power, but not for the same reason as his father. He wanted order and peace, not to see more people he cared about die.

"There's no point in being the king of New York if everyone hates you," Caesar said under his breath and took a bite of his food.

"Come again?" Cassius raised a brow.

"Nothing," Caesar sighed.

"Good. For a second there I thought that you were going against me."

"Nasir . . . do you trust him?"

"With my life," Cassius said and looked at the diamond watch on his wrist. "Shit. I'm going to be late."

"For what?"

"Business," Cassius said, taking a big bite of his sandwich. A glob of jelly fell onto his shirt, staining it. "Dammit!"

"I'll go with you," Caesar suggested.

"No, no. I need you to go upstate with Niles and collect some money for me."

"You're sending me on penny duty?"

"If fifty thousand dollars is penny duty."

"Who the hell owes us fifty grand?"

"White boy named Raymond. I gave him some product to take to a buyer in Rochester weeks ago and haven't heard from him since. The buyer hasn't either. One of them is lying to me. I need you and Niles to figure out who it is."

"Got it."

"And have Pricilla get me a new shirt. I got this damned jelly all over me."

"I guess that maybe now isn't the best time to tell you that I fired both her and Amira today because Amira and I are together. Wow, would you look at the time. I better head over to Niles's house." Caesar jumped up and hurried to leave the kitchen.

"Caesar! Wait!"

Caesar cursed under his breath and slowly turned around to face his father. He thought he was going to find disappointment there, but instead he saw the hint of a smile.

"Yeah?"

"I love you."

"I love you too."

"I know you're not all the way on board with this shit, but I appreciate you for standing beside me. You're growing up to be a be a good man, probably a better man than I'll ever be. But one day you'll see that I'm making the right decision for us."

Caesar didn't know what to say, so he just nodded and waved goodbye.

Never let your left hand know what your right is up to.

Chapter 8

"Well, ain't you just the smoothest nigga I done ever laid eyes on!"

Caesar found himself grinning when his cousin Niles got into the BMW. Niles was only two years older than him and was known for talking mess. A brown corduroy cabbie hat rested on top of his short 'fro, and he wore the matching brown bell bottoms. Niles was what men would call a high yella Negro and what the girls would call "dreamy." He had a muscular build and was a damned good shot. The two of them tried to keep each other out of trouble as much as possible.

"Seat belt," Caesar said before he pulled away from in front of Niles's home.

"Oh, yeah, I heard about ya run-in with the law. You on the straight and narrow now, is that it?" Niles poked fun at him.

"You won't be talking all that shit if I get into an accident and you fly through this window, will you?"

"Hell no, nigga! I'd be dead!" Niles said seriously, and Caesar laughed again. "But no, seriously, cousin, what the fuck?"

"Man, I got caught slipping."

"Kings don't get caught slipping. What happened?"

"It was that motherfucka Gerald. He set me up. That bastard was working with the Feds."

"See! See! What the hell did I tell you?"

"You know what you told me."

"Nah, nah. I wanna hear you say it. What the fuck did I tell you?"

"You told me Gerald wasn't no good."

"Exactly. I know a dirty-ass motherfucka when I see one. But the good thing is you're out."

"You know my pops came to the rescue."

"I know that's right. Learn from that lesson, Caes man. I know you wanna see everybody eat and all, but some motherfuckas you gotta just give scraps to."

"I hear you."

"But do you really?"

"I hear you!"

"A'ight, man. I don't got time for ya daddy to be comin' and tryin'a ram his size eleven up my ass because of some shit you did."

"Man, shut up. Did he tell you all the details about what we're doing today?"

"Yup. I know exactly where we're goin', too. I'm the one who dropped the coke off to Raymond."

"And who the fuck is Raymond anyway?" Caesar asked, scrunching his face up. "And why haven't I ever heard of him?"

"You have. You just don't know him as Raymond. You know him as Money Man."

"Shut the fuck up. Money Man owes us fifty?"

"*Fifty,*" Niles confirmed, shaking his head. "He was supposed to run that shit to the buyer and bring back the money. But somehow the money *and* the drugs are MIA."

Money Man had been doing business with the Kings for some years. He had even brought them a few of their best customers. He was a corporate man, but Caesar had only gotten to know him by his alias in their dealings together. He worked for some pharmaceutical company, which was how he was able to connect them with clients.

"Let's hope he has a real good explanation behind all of this."

"Fuck an explanation. He better have the money or the drugs when we get there, or it's lights out for Money Man."

Caesar nodded his head in agreement. Niles directed him the rest of the way until they reached a high-rise condo. They parked on the street outside of it, and Caesar looked up.

"What floor?" he asked.

"Tenth."

"You sure he's in there? If I owed somebody fifty thousand and they knew where I lived, I for damn sure wouldn't come home."

"That slimy bastard has been doing his best to duck us, but one of my guys said they saw him come home last night."

"Okay then, let's boogie." Caesar reached across to the glove compartment and pulled out a revolver pistol. He checked to make sure it was loaded before tucking it under his jacket and into his pants.

When they got out of the car, the two men got a lot of stares from the women walking up and down the sidewalk. There was one in particular who was eyeing Niles down. She was cute and wore a straight wig that was flipped at the ends. In her hands were bags, indicating that she was out on a shopping spree. But the way she was looking at Niles, she was out looking for more than just clothes and shoes. She licked her lips at him and made a "come here" motion with her finger.

"Look at that fine thang right there. I would let her eat this dick all up," Niles said, winking at her.

"That's not what we're here for."

"I know, nigga. I can look though, can't I?"

They got to the revolving doors of the condo and stepped inside. The doorman was busy giving a tenant a package and didn't even notice them slide by to the elevators. Niles pressed the button for the tenth floor, and up they went.

"Did your people say if Money Man was by himself?"

"No, why?"

"Because if you owed the most dangerous man in New York fifty thousand dollars, would you be alone?"

"I didn't think of that."

"Of course you didn't. Be ready for anything."

When the elevator let them off, Caesar followed Niles to a door in the middle of the wide hallway. Niles motioned silently at the door, and Caesar nodded. He looked over his shoulder before drawing his gun and waited for Niles's knuckles to hit the door.

Knock! Knock!

When they heard footsteps approach, they both stepped out of the way of the peephole.

"Who's there?" The voice was gruff, and Caesar didn't recognize it.

"Is Raymond here?" Niles asked.

"Whose askin'?"

"I'm Bill, his neighbor from down the hall," Niles said in his best Caucasian hippie imitation. "I heard he was who to come to for pills and shit, man. But if he doesn't want my money—"

The door unlocked before Niles even finished speaking, and a big white man revealed himself. Once the entrance was big enough to go through, Caesar shoved his gun in the man's face and ran inside the condo. Niles moved quickly behind him, aiming his pistol at the rest of the house.

"Hands where I can see them, motherfuckas, or I'ma turn you all into spaghetti!" Niles shouted.

The three men sitting in the all-white living room stopped and put their hands in the air. The blunt that was in rotation fell to the floor. Caesar pushed his man against the wall and snatched the firearm from his hip, tucking it into his own pants. Feeling that he might prove to be a problem, Caesar took the liberty of hitting him hard in the temple with the revolver, knocking him out cold.

"He's in here," Niles called over his shoulder to Caesar.

After Caesar made sure the front door was locked, he stepped over the unconscious man and went to the living room. Sure enough, there was Money Man looking like a million bucks. His hair was combed back, and he was dressed in a Versace suit and had two gold rings on his right hand. The sight of Caesar brought the most uneasy look to Money Man's face.

"Money Man, just the person I came to see. Niles, check them all for guns," Caesar instructed.

Caesar aimed his weapon at them and watched like a hawk for even a twitch while Niles disarmed them. When all their weapons were placed on the kitchen table a ways away, Niles came back and stood next to him. It was then that Caesar took notice of the stacks of money on the glass coffee table in front of the men, along with lines of cocaine and weed.

"Caesar, man. I was coming to see Cassius today to drop off his money."

"Is that right? Because it looks like you were smoking and having a good time to me. What you think, Niles?"

"I'm thinking that better either be our money or coke on this here table," Niles answered.

"What happened Money Man? You were supposed to drop that off for us, but we haven't heard from you. Did you even take it to Rochester like you were supposed to?"

"Of course I did," Money Man answered.

"Okay, that's one mystery solved. Now on to the next. Where's our fucking money?"

"Caesar, listen, I was going to bring you your money. I swear," Money Man said, putting his palms up.

"Then explain why you have all this muscle around you. You've never had security before. Why now?"

"Because he knew we were gonna come for his ass, that's why," Niles said.

"What happened, Money Man?" Caesar inquired again.

Money Man looked from one gun to the other before he groaned loudly. "All right, all right. I fucked up, okay? I fucked up."

"So you *didn't* drop the drugs off?"

"No, I did. But when I got all that money in my hands, I went a little wild. That's all."

"You spent it?"

"A little of it."

"Okay, so how much is left?"

"That." Money Man slowly looked at the money on the coffee table.

"You gotta be fuckin' kiddin' me!" Niles exclaimed. "Motherfucka, that don't look to be more than ten thousand dollars."

"It's almost twenty. I'll get the thirty for you."

Caesar took a deep breath and blew the air out through his mouth. His head fell back for a second, and he tried to calm the sea of anger about to surface. He wished Money Man had told him something other than what he just had.

"You've been doing business with us all this time. Why would you fuck up now?"

"Cassius never gave me a job this big before."

"He thought you had proved yourself trustworthy. That word, trust. He's very big on that. Especially since he doesn't give his away easily."

"I might have gone a little overboard, but—"

"A little? You spent thirty thousand fucking dollars! And cut the bullshit. You weren't planning on paying us back. If you were, you would have done it by now."

"What you wanna do with this sorry-ass piece of shit, Caes?" Niles asked.

"The same thing we do to any other snake that slithers its way into our garden. Cut its head off."

Caesar had every intention of putting a bullet in Money Man's skull right then and there, but he noticed one of the other men make a move for his ankle. He pulled out a small handgun and was fixing to aim it at an unsuspecting Niles. Caesar had to react fast. He averted his aim from Money Man and shot his accomplice in his temple. The man's head snapped to the side, but it was just the diversion the other accomplice needed to tackle Caesar to the ground. Niles tried to shoot him, but Money Man punched him in the face.

The man on top of Caesar knocked the revolver away and wrapped his hands around Caesar's neck. Gasping for air, Caesar reached for his pocket and withdrew a small switchblade from it. His strength was leaving him, but he used the last of it to shove the knife into the man's red neck. He collapsed, choking on his own blood, and Caesar stood rockily to his feet, trying to catch his breath. When he did, he saw Niles and Money Man in the middle of a full-on fist fight. Caesar spotted his revolver and picked it up. The moment he got a clear shot, he took it. The bullet lodged itself in Money Man's skull and made him drop instantly.

"Man! What you do that for? I was whoopin' his ass!" Niles exclaimed.

"No, you were wasting time. Grab that money. We gotta go. I'm sure one of the neighbors heard the gunshots!"

Niles came back to the King mansion with Caesar. Caesar didn't know if his father had returned home yet, but just in case he had, he didn't want to be alone in telling him the news about Money Man. Cassius was never happy about losing money. But at least that time it hadn't been a mistake made on Caesar's part. He also knew Cassius would be happy to learn that Money Man was dead. He wasn't the type of man who would let someone redeem themselves after wronging him. Once you proved yourself disloyal, that was all she wrote.

"You boys want some lunch?" Martina asked when they came into the kitchen.

"Yes, please. I'm starvin'!" Niles told her, leaning on the island. He turned to Caesar, who had taken a seat on a barstool next to him. "And you think you're slick comin' here instead of takin' me home."

"I don't know what you're talking about." Caesar feigned innocence.

"Nigga, please. Didn't I just tell you earlier that I don't want ya daddy's foot up my ass? He's gon' be pissed off when we tell him this shit!"

"Y'all know I don't like all that cursing in my kitchen, now!" Martina chastised, pointing a spatula their way.

"I'm sorry, Miss Martina," Niles said, trying to offer her a smile, but she squinted her eyes at him. He turned back to Caesar with wide eyes and whispered, "She used to be nice."

"She still is. I just don't think she likes you."

"Whatever, man. Where is Cassius anyways?"

"I don't know. He said he had some business to handle. I'm sure he'll be back soon enough."

The phone on the kitchen wall rang, and Martina stopped cooking to answer it. Niles was cracking another joke about what Cassius was going to do to them when Martina waved the phone at Caesar.

"It's for you, Caesar honey," she said, stretching the cord over the island to hand it to him.

"Hello?"

"Caesar King?"

"Nasir?" Caesar asked, recognizing the deep voice. "My dad is out right now."

"I'm not calling for him. I'm calling about him." There was something about the way he said it that made Caesar's stomach turn.

"What is it. Does he need me?"

"No. I don't know how to tell you this, kid, but Cassius is dead."

Chapter 9

The Present

Caesar took what felt like the biggest breath of his life, and he attempted to pull himself together. He stared at the revolving door of the hospital and watched people rushing in and out, knowing that when he left, he might not ever be the same again. A hand gently touched his shoulder, and he turned his attention to his companion. Diana gave him a sad smile and urged him to follow her.

"We have to go in now, Caesar," she said, and he nodded.

"I know. I'm just not ready."

"Me either, but this is just one of those things that we have to do. We have each other to lean on. Come on. Before security has us removed for loitering."

She led the way into the hospital and to the pathology department. The closer they got, the more Caesar's chest seemed to cave. Losing his wife had been unbearable, and losing Barry had been another blow. But when he received the call that Boogie had been killed, it was like whatever life Caesar had left went with him. Boogie had become like a son to him. He loved him. Caesar couldn't help but wonder if he had cheated death just for it to be dealt to the next person.

"How can I help you today?" the receptionist asked.

"We're here to view a body," Diana answered. "Bryshon Tolliver."

The receptionist typed something into her computer, and when she found what she was looking for, she pursed her lips. She looked from the screen and then back at the two of them.

"It looks like someone already identified the body. They were able to give the police a positive ID when he was first brought in almost forty-eight hours ago."

"I don't think you heard me right. We're here to view the body, not identify it," Diana told her with a straight face. "We are his next of kin, so I'm not sure why anyone else would have been called to identify him. Find someone to take us to him."

The receptionist paused, visibly flustered. But it was as if she knew denying Diana what she wanted wouldn't be in her best interest. She paged someone, and a few minutes later a man wearing a pair of scrubs came to the front.

"Anna, you paged?" he asked the receptionist.

"Yes, I did, John. These people would like to view the body of the shooting victim who was brought in two days ago."

"He was already identified."

"I know. That's what I, um, that's what I said."

John turned to face Diana and Caesar. They both wore determined expressions that let him know they weren't leaving until they got what they came for. John sighed and looked around the empty lobby and nodded his head.

"I don't see what harm it will do. I understand these things can be very unsettling. Was he your son?"

"Yes," Caesar answered without batting an eye.

"Right this way." John motioned for them to follow him.

He led them to the morgue. The room reeked of death, but that didn't move Caesar. The only thing on his mind was saying goodbye to Boogie.

"Tolliver," John said as he approached a cold locker. "There you are."

He pulled the body out, and Caesar clenched his jaw as he stared at the thin white sheet that covered it. He approached slowly, and John stepped back.

"I was on my way to the lab to grab something when Anna paged me. Technically I'm not supposed to do this, but if I leave you here for a few moments, do you promise not to steal any bodies?"

"What?" Diana turned her lip up at him.

"Right, wrong time to make a joke," John said and widened his eyes. "I'll be right back."

He left the two of them standing in front of the open locker. Caesar kept urging his hand to pull the sheet back, but something was getting lost in translation. He found himself reflecting on the time he and Boogie stood over Barry's body to identify him. Whatever feelings Boogie had been feeling then, staring down at his own father's lifeless body, were the same ones Caesar wanted to avoid. He wasn't ready to see Boogie like that. However, that was the reason he came. He had to see for himself that Boogie was really dead.

He balled the corner of the sheet into his fist and pulled the sheet back. Beside him he heard Diana take a sharp breath. Her hand flew to her chest as they stared down at the body. Caesar's eyes first went to the bullet holes in his pale chest. There was no way anyone could have survived a direct hit like that. The next thing he looked at was Boogie's face, only to find that there wasn't a thing about it that he recognized. The man on the table was about the same age as Boogie, but he in fact was *not* him.

"What in the world . . ." Diana whispered, seeing the same thing as Caesar. "Maybe the mortician pulled the wrong body."

"He said the name Tolliver when he pulled this one out," Caesar said and curiously checked the toe tag. "And this here says this man's name is Bryshon Tolliver, but I think we can both agree that this isn't Boogie."

"They said someone positively identified him. Who could have done that?"

"Good! You're here!" a familiar voice sounded almost on cue.

Both Caesar and Diana turned to the door in unison and found Caesar's nephew Nicky standing at the morgue's entrance. He wore fresh braids and street clothes. He also seemed out of breath, like he had run all the way down there. Nicky had been the one who informed Caesar about the shooting. If Caesar had been in his right mind when he got off the plane, he would have called his nephew the moment he touched down. However, his mind was so clouded that he hadn't even thought to.

"Nicky! What are you doing here?"

"I've been trying to reach both of you for hours! When you didn't return my messages, I took a wild guess of where I might find you."

"Is this some kind of sick joke, Nicky?" Caesar asked with frustration dripping from each word. "You said Boogie was dead, but this isn't Boogie."

"I can explain everything. A lot of shit has happened. But first we need to get out of here."

"No, I'm not spending another second without knowing what the hell is going on around me. They said they got a positive ID on Boogie's body, and I want to see him before I leave."

"Boogie's body isn't here. I'm the one who positively identified whoever that John Doe is and said he was Boogie."

"Why would you do something like that?"

"To keep Boogie safe," Nicky answered, and Caesar's heart almost stopped.

"To keep him safe? You say that like he's alive."

"He is, but we had to keep a low profile. With Zo's crazy-ass aunt still somewhere lurking around, and Roz's crazy baby daddy—"

"Who?" Diana asked.

"Like I said, it's a lot. And we didn't want to take any chances. Right now, anyone affiliated with Zo has a target on their back. So, Unc, please put that nigga back on ice, and let's go to the Big House."

"Wait. The Big House?" Diana asked, confused. "The location was compromised. Why would we go there? It isn't safe."

"I guess I should say the new Big House." Nicky grinned sheepishly at them. "After Roz was shot, Boogie decided to take a page out of Caesar's book. He had a house built on uncharted property on the outskirts of the city. Only we know the location of it. Now come on. He's waiting for you."

Chapter 10

The Big House that Boogie had built was a gigantic and beautiful property. It too was brick, but it had an old-world vibe about it. There were even gargoyle statues perched on the top of it. Caesar would have to take time another day to truly admire it and take it all in. But when he burst through the front doors, the only thing he cared to see was his godson. He didn't have to search very far to find him. Together in the large sitting area on the first level of the home were Morgan, Roz, Nathan, and Tazz. They were all gathered around a very worn out–looking Boogie. His chest and shoulder were wrapped in white bandages, and he was obviously drained. However, his eyes lit up when he saw Diana rushing to him. She pushed Morgan, who'd been sitting next to him, out of the way and sat down.

"Oh, Boogie!" she exclaimed and touched his face softly. Warm tears fell down her cheekbones. "I thought we lost you."

"I did too, but luckily for me, the man who shot me wasn't a real shooter. One of the bullets he hit me with was a flesh wound and the other lodged in my shoulder. I lost a lot of blood waiting for the ambulance to come though. I thought it was over for me."

Caesar took a seat across from them even though what he really wanted to do was pull Boogie into a tight embrace. However, when the two men connected eyes, his relief to see the young man was translated. He gave Boogie a small smile and was given a nod in response.

"I'm glad to see that you're still here in the land of the living," Caesar told him.

"It's going to take more than something like this to take me out."

"Well, either way you should be resting! Why isn't he in bed?" Diana asked, and her piercing gaze went around the room.

"We have been telling him to lie down and get his strength back. But he won't listen!" Morgan explained.

"I can't lie down and rest. Not when that motherfucka has my daughter," Boogie said through clenched teeth.

"Amber? Somebody took Amber?" Diana's alarmed eyes turned to Roz, who tearfully nodded her head. "Who?"

"Her birth father." Roz's voice shook when she spoke. "After he shot Boogie, he stole her from me."

"And he'll die for it," Boogie growled.

"Boogie, you have to focus on getting some rest—" Morgan started, but Boogie interrupted her.

"I'll rest when I'm dead. And I'm not. Y'all should already know how I'm about to get down. Between Adam and Louisa, they got us looking like some clowns in our own domain. I won't stand for it. Not after we've come so far."

"Well, you won't be any good to us if you don't let yourself get back to one hundred percent," Nicky butted in.

"What part about 'that nigga has my daughter' don't you understand?" Boogie growled.

"I understand every word. And if you think we aren't scouring the city looking for any trace of them, then you're a fool."

Caesar cleared his throat before Boogie could say anything else, and everyone shifted their attention to him.

"I know there are a lot of emotions swirling around the room right now, but there are a few blind spots for me that I need filled in. I thought the situation with Marco's sister was handled."

"We thought so too. But apparently it isn't. Louisa was madder than we thought at Lorenzo for turning down her offer. And from the looks of it, she recruited Adam in the process. She also . . ."

"What?"

"Daniella wasn't as fortunate as me. Louisa killed her." Boogie swallowed.

"No." Caesar felt a genuine sadness for Christina, Marco's wife.

"It was bad," Nicky said, shaking his head, and Caesar sighed.

"How did she come to know Adam?"

"She was following us. She had to have been," Boogie said like it was something he'd been pondering. "She used Adam's hate for me to infiltrate our operation seamlessly."

"All because Lorenzo told her no?" It wasn't adding up to Caesar.

"Right before Boogie was shot, she basically said she blames all of us for Marco's death," Morgan explained. "She said he was the only thing she ever loved."

Her words stung Caesar, mainly because he blamed himself for Marco dying. Although his old friend knew what their kind of lifestyle came with, he died because of his loyalty to Caesar. And if his death was what the new ring of chaos was stemming from, then Caesar figured he would have to be the one who put it right.

"She also said that none of us are competent enough to run a business and everybody would know it soon," Nicky added. "And that's just what we need right? Another motherfucka tryin'a blow up the spot."

"All of this back-to-back feuding is reminding me of the old days when my father controlled Harlem," Diana said to Caesar.

"Well, I refuse to lose anybody else before we find a common ground. Where's Lorenzo? Is he here?" Caesar looked around.

"No." Nicky shook his head. "If Louisa is somewhere still lurking around, he doesn't want us in danger because of his presence. He feels like it's his fault that Boogie got shot."

"Nobody is at fault except the ones opposing us. Not working together is what has caused all this turmoil. One family is already missing from the fold, but we're still here, and that's going to count for something. Let me handle Louisa."

"Her operation is strong, Caesar," Diana reminded him.

"And ours is stronger. Marco may have allowed her to believe her position with us was higher than it actually was, but I won't make that mistake. Before I go, Boogie, let me help you to bed."

"I can do that, Caesar." Roz hurried to her feet when Caesar got up.

"No, I insist." Caesar raised his brows at her, and she nodded her understanding. "Everyone except Tazz needs to be out there trying to locate Adam and Amber. I want her brought home, and I want his head, understand?"

"Got it," Nicky and Nathan said in unison.

"Understood. I am about to go meet with Bentley and see what he's come up with," Morgan said.

"I'll go with you." Diana stood up and grabbed her purse. "Caesar, call me later."

When they left, Caesar and Boogie left Tazz and Roz in the sitting room. Caesar helped Boogie to the elevator at the end of a hallway, and he could tell that the short walk had taken a lot out of him. He was also trying to hide the pain in his shoulder. However, when he brushed it against the door when he stepped inside, Caesar saw him wince. The elevator took them to the second level of the house, and when they stepped off, there was a wheelchair a few steps away.

"Sit down," Caesar instructed.

"I'm good. I can walk."

"Where's your room?"

"There," Boogie said and pointed to double doors at the end of the hall.

"Boy, if you don't get your ass in this chair. Stop being stubborn."

Boogie grumbled a little bit, but he did as he was told. Caesar knew the strong exterior was due to the soldier in him. Boogie needed to know that it was okay to let the people around him take care of him. He didn't always have to be the strongest in the room. When they got to the room, Caesar helped him onto the bed and placed a blanket over him.

"You should really have a nurse taking care of you," Caesar told him.

"Nicky nabbed me some pain medication after I got out of surgery."

"Surgery?"

"When they rushed me to the hospital, they did emergency surgery to remove the bullets. When I was stable enough, Nicky swapped me out with a body with similar wounds."

"That was the smart thing to do, but you should still have a nurse here to make sure the entry points don't get infected."

"I'll be my own nurse. Trust me when I say these aren't the first bullet wounds I've tended to. I don't need to remind you who my dad was."

"You got me there," Caesar chuckled and then grew serious again. "You know, when I . . . when I heard something had happened to you, I . . . can't describe the sorrow I felt. It hit me then how much you mean to me. I wasn't able to keep Barry alive, but I'll be damned if you leave the same way as him. We may not be bound by blood, but you are a son to me."

To his words Boogie had none. A silence fell over them, and Boogie turned away, pretending he had gotten something in his eye. Caesar would never say it out loud, but he saw the single tear Boogie wiped away. He himself had a ball in his throat that he had to swallow. He patted Boogie on the hand and made to leave, but a tight grip on his wrist stopped him.

"Wait, I wanted to ask you somethin'," Boogie said, finally finding his voice. He let go of Caesar's wrist when he sat back down.

"Anything."

"I just feel like this chaos is becomin' the new normal. I hate it. Every time I think shit is smooth sailing, some more bullshit comes out of the dark. It's brought the people still standin' closer, but it's fuckin' with business. And that's what will draw us apart. I don't know what to do."

"So ask your question," Caesar said, and Boogie looked befuddled.

"I just told you that I don't know what to do!"

"That's not a question."

"How?"

"Because it was a statement."

"No, not that. I'm askin', how did you do it? How did you bring a peace that lasted so long?"

"I never have told you the story of how the pact came to be, have I?" Caesar sighed. "I guess we have some time now. It all started when my father died . . ."

Light will outshine all darkness.

Chapter 11

The Past

Caesar sat in the front pew of the church by himself, staring at his father's golden casket. He had never before experienced a chest cave like that one, and although he was surrounded by family, he had never felt so alone. He now was an orphan. No mother and no father. His father had been found by a dock with ten bullets in his body. He had bled out, and the part that made Caesar the saddest was knowing that he had died alone.

As the reverend spoke to the congregation, Caesar felt hands squeezing his shoulder. He could feel the love in the pressure, but love wouldn't bring Cassius back. He held back his tears and kept his eyes glued to the closed casket. Cassius's body was actually suitable for viewing, being that it was his entire torso that had been shot up. However, Caesar wouldn't allow anyone to see his father in death. He wanted their only memories of him to be of when he was alive. The Cassius King. Forever.

"Death is always a sad thing," the reverend's voice boomed. "But let me remind all of you that although Brother King had his ways, the light of God outshines all darkness. He forgives all sins, and only He has the say-so on who walks through those pearly gates. I know in my heart that Cassius King is walking with our Maker alongside his wife and looking down on his only son. Caesar, you are and forever will be covered, you hear? You don't just have one guardian angel. Now you have two. I hope you find solace in that. I'm going to be praying on your healing."

There was clapping, and a few amens were shouted from behind Caesar. But although the reverend's words were heartfelt, they didn't fill the void Caesar had in his soul. Thinking about his parents in heaven did nothing but remind him that they were gone. They were dead, and he was alone. He sat through the rest of the funeral service, and when it was time to leave, he helped the other pallbearers carry the casket to the hearse. Afterward, Caesar rode with Niles to the grave site.

"I'm not gonna ask you no stupid-ass questions about whether you're okay," Niles said, breaking the silence after a while of driving behind the hearse.

"It sounds a little like you're asking," Caesar said.

"Nah. Because I know you're not okay. Shit, I'm not okay. This here fucked me up in the head, man."

"I . . . I just don't know what to do."

"Well, I'll tell you what you can't do, and that's show weakness. Anybody else would be able to shed a few tears for their daddy bein' killed. But you? Nah. You just acquired the biggest drug operation in New York City. You have to be a shark. We still don't know who did it?"

"No. And forensics confirmed yesterday that his body wasn't moved from somewhere else. He died where he was found."

"And there was nobody else around?" Niles asked.

"*Nobody,*" Caesar confirmed, and the two of them exchanged a look.

They didn't speak another word inside the car. They'd reached the burial site, and it was time to say final goodbyes. Cassius had always been a meticulous man and had planned every detail of his own funeral after his wife died. The thing he had been most adamant about was being buried next to her. After they carried the casket to the freshly dug hole, they placed it on the lowering device. Everyone besides Caesar stepped back and waited for the last of the cars to come. Amira was among them, and he watched as she aided her grandmother up the hill. When she and Caesar connected eyes, she offered him an encouraging smile and blew him a kiss. He was glad she was there. When everyone had arrived, he looked around and let his eyes fall on Ed and Joseph, Cassius's oldest friends and bodyguards. Their eyes were red, and Caesar knew it was because they'd been crying. His family comforted them with hugs and pats on the back. It was truly a sad occasion.

In the back of the crowd, Caesar's eyes were surprised to fall on one face: Nasir's. Not too far behind him were a few of his bodyguards, and when he saw Caesar's eyes on him, he nodded respectfully. Caesar returned the gesture and waited until white roses were handed out to everyone before he began speaking.

"My father stated in his will that he would want a small gathering with only his family. But I think he forgot how big his family actually is." Caesar smiled, and everyone around him shared a laugh. "I feel that the reverend said all the good stuff, so there isn't much more to it. But what I will say is mostly everyone here knows what kind of man Cassius King was—cutthroat but loyal. And the one thing he loved most was family. What he built most men only dream about. I see many of you arrived today in nice cars, wearing designer clothes, and shining because of the jewels on your necks and wrists. Bellies so full that you might not even need to go to the repast. And it's no secret that the reason behind you having all these things is my father, Cassius King. He created an empire with jobs and opportunity for all of you. As I said before, he loved you. And I hope that even now you never forget that. His death is what I would like to call untimely, but his legacy will live on through me."

Caesar stopped addressing them and focused on the casket. He placed his single white rose on top of it, wanting to say his personal goodbye while Cassius was still above ground. But when it came time to speak, no words came out. He remembered the last conversation he had with his father and realized that he'd already said goodbye. So instead, he kissed three of his fingers and placed them on the casket before walking away back to Niles's car.

As he stood and waited for Niles to finish mingling with the family, Amira approached him. She threw her arms around his shoulder and hugged him tightly before letting go. Staring up into his eyes, concern dripped from hers.

"I'll be all right," Caesar said, answering the question her lips had yet to ask.

"Caesar, your father just died. It's okay to be sad."

"Who said I'm not sad? I'm tormented. But these are the cards I was dealt, and I'm still in the game, so I have to play."

"But this is your family. You can let your guard down around them."

"That would be nice, but no, thank you."

"Why do you have to be so tough all the time?" Amira asked, kissing his chin.

"Because my father raised me to be strong even in a time of weakness. The family you're telling me to let my guard down in front of are the same ones who never wanted me running any kind of business. And now I'm the one in charge of all these motherfuckas."

"I get it, I really do. You have to mourn in your own way, but make sure you do. Or else it will come out in the worst ways."

"I hear you," Caesar told her.

Niles had come back to the car by then, and he had Pricilla holding on to his elbow. The black veil connected to her hat covered most of her face, but Caesar could still see the tear streaks on the bottoms of her cheeks.

"Come on, Amira," Pricilla said, switching from Niles's arm to Amira's. "I want to make it back to the mansion and make sure everything is in order before all these people get there."

"Oh, you don't have to worry about any of that, Ms. Pricilla. Martina and the others have it all covered," Caesar tried to tell her.

"Martina?" Pricilla scoffed. "That woman couldn't find her left shoe if it was on her foot! Now I won't let Mr. King's homegoing be a mess now. Oh no. Not Mr. King's homegoing. That man liked everything a certain way, and I'm going to make sure it's *his* way, understand? Now come on, Amira! Before Martina pulls out the wrong glasses.

Mr. King would turn over in that nice casket if he knew these people were drinking out of the glasses he imported from France!"

"Okay, Grandma," Amira said and grabbed her hand. She turned back to Caesar and blew him another kiss. "I'll see you there."

When they were gone, Caesar and Niles leaned on the car and watched as one by one people cleared out of the burial site. When only a handful of people were left, Ed and Joseph included, Caesar watched them in silence.

"You ready to head back to the house?" Niles asked. When Caesar didn't answer, he studied the thoughtful expression on his face. "Hey, Caesar, you good?"

"I need you to set up a meeting for me tomorrow."

"Caesar, we just buried Cassius. Take a second to—"

"It's important, Niles," Caesar said seriously, finally breaking his gaze from the two men.

"Fine." Niles sighed reluctantly. "Who do you need to see?"

"Damián Alverez."

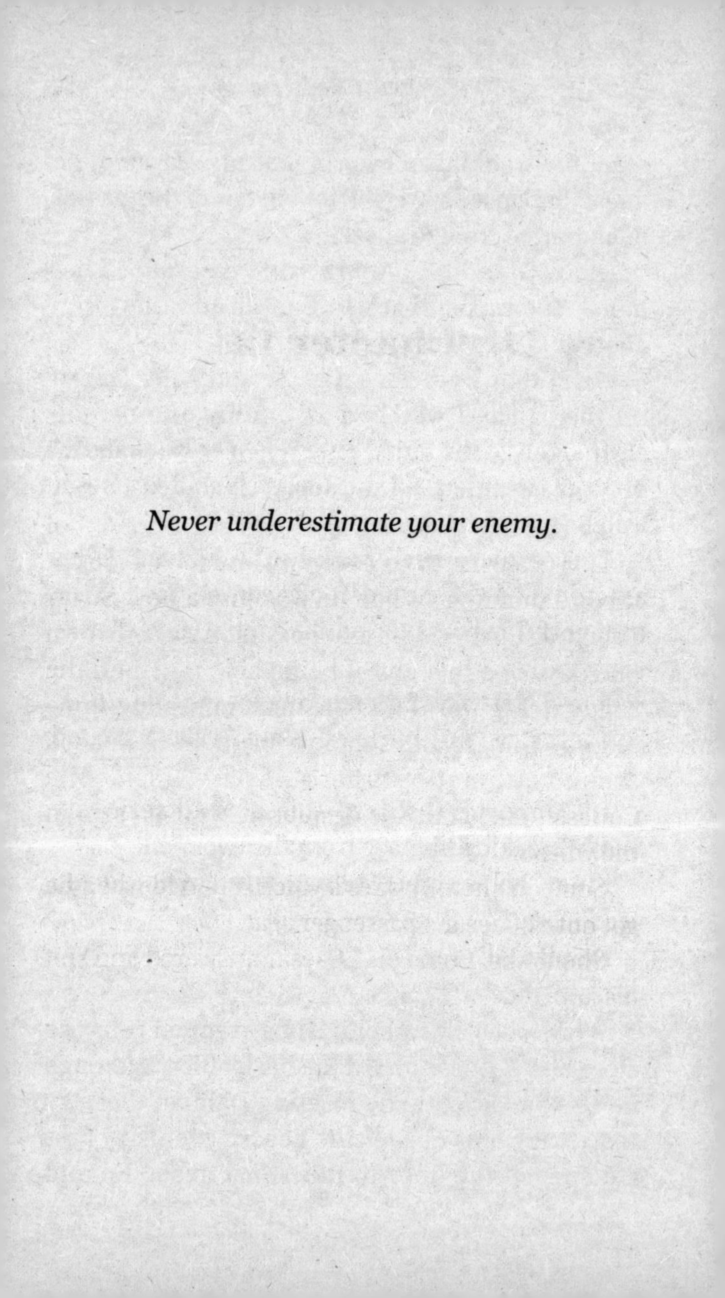

Never underestimate your enemy.

Chapter 12

It was midday when Caesar got to Sugar Land, the candy store he now owned along with everything else that was once his father's. He got out of his car, chewing a piece of gum, and took a look at the old building. When he was just a boy, Sugar Land was the business that he couldn't wait to own one day. The thought of being able to eat all the candy in the world was the most appealing thing to him. Things were simple back then. He looked around and noticed there was an Oldsmobile Cutlass parked outside despite the CLOSED sign in the window.

"Someone here?" Niles's voice sounded when he got out of Caesar's passenger seat.

"Should be. Come on," Caesar answered and spit his gum out.

With Niles close behind, he stepped into the store and headed toward the back office. Although he was supposed to be meeting Damián that day, there were a few people he needed to talk to first. He opened the door to the office to see Ed and

Joseph waiting impatiently for him. They were seated against the wall on the lime green sofa that Cassius had seemed to love so much.

"Ed, Joseph! I wasn't expectin' to see you two here," Niles stated, genuinely taken aback.

"Well, I for one wasn't expectin' to be here. I have important business to tend to, so I hope you plan on makin' this snappy, Caesar."

Joseph didn't try to hide the irritation in his tone, and Caesar didn't like that. The way he spoke was in a way he would never dare to speak to Cassius. Caesar inhaled an even breath and offered them a smile. He took a seat at his father's desk, and Niles stood beside it.

"I called you two here today because I know you two used to be my father's closest friends. I just wanted to ask you if you know anything about who might have done this to him."

"Instead of askin' us, you should be out there tryin' to find his killers yourself," Ed said in the same kind of condescending tone as Joseph.

"That's what I'm trying to do right now. Since the two of you were his friends and bodyguards, I figured I would start with you. What were his moves the day he was killed?"

The two men glanced at each other before Ed sighed. "We were gonna handle it ourselves," he said.

"Handle what?"

"Get back."

"Explain."

"The day your father died, he took us with him to meet with the Mexicans. We told him it was a bad idea, that there was too much blood in the field for it to be safe. But he wouldn't listen."

"Caesar, you of all people should know how hardheaded Cassius could be when his mind was set to somethin'," Joseph chimed in. "And he was set on controllin' the five families. He'd been talkin' about it for months. He was convinced that once it was done, it would make him the most powerful man on the whole East Coast."

"Because it would have," Caesar stated, and Joseph nodded.

"This is true. But he was talkin' about a hostile takeover from people who had the same God complex as him. It was a crazy idea, but he thought he could pull it off especially with the Mexicans being under Fed radar. He thought they would come over quietly. I loved Cassius like a brother, but his thirst for ultimate power led him down the wrong rabbit hole and to a snake."

"So you're saying that the Mexicans murdered my father?"

"That's what you heard, isn't it?" Joseph asked. "I say we hit them where it hurts."

He and Ed stared at Caesar like he was stupid. The vibe they were giving off was cold, and it was one he'd never felt from them before. In fact, they shared the same look of outright dislike of him at the moment.

"I think that before any rash decisions are made, we should explore all our options."

"What other option could it be?" Ed exclaimed and threw his hands up into the air. "He met with the Mexicans and wound up dead. It ain't rocket science what needs to be done, but maybe for you it is. I always told Cassius that you were too naive to be in charge. You don't have the gall to do what needs to be done to take Cassius's place. In fact—"

"You better think wisely on the words you're about to say," Niles warned him, and the men glared at each other.

"It's all right, Niles. Let him say what he was going to say. In fact what, Ed?" Caesar made a circular motion with his hand, urging Ed to continue.

"We don't think you're the right or smart choice to take over for Cassius."

"Oh, really? Then who is?"

"Someone who's been here since you were in diapers. You can run the legitimate side of the operation like a good boy. But the heavy stuff will be left to us. Plus, you have to know that the only reason the others in the operation listened to you was because Cassius was alive. What do you think they're gonna do now? You're just a kid."

"I don't need to explain to you my qualifications to run my father's entire operation. I also don't care about who agrees with you about said qualifications not being good enough to run *my* family legacy. Understand? The flawed will always fold, and the loyal will never waver."

"It isn't about waverin'. It's about makin' an executive decision. And it's been made. You're out, Caesar."

"You probably really believe that, don't you?" Caesar asked.

"I know it," Ed said as he and Joseph exchanged a look.

At the same time, they began to laugh. It was a sinister laugh, one that said they'd put Caesar in his place. To them he was just a little boy who could be easily bullied since his father wasn't around. But it was that same little boy's laughter joining theirs that made them stop.

"You know," Caesar said, still laughing, "the show you put on yesterday at the funeral was almost believable. The tears were a great touch. I want to double back on the sentence I started with when I said I know the two of you used to be my father's closest friends. I just want to know when that changed."

"What the hell are you talkin' about?" Ed spat.

"You know exactly what I'm talking about."

"We grew up with Cassius. He was one of our greatest friends."

"Then why the fuck are the two of you sitting in front of me. Living . . . breathing . . . when my dad is dead? The two of you don't even have a scrape or bruise on your body. If you were there, how could that be?"

"Their aim was off that day." Joseph lowered his eyelids at Caesar.

"Aim was off, that's a good one. Okay, then answer me this—does the business that you so greatly need to tend to entail going to all of my father's stash spots and cleaning out the safes?"

"What?" Niles's eyes grew wide as he looked from Caesar to the other two.

Joseph's and Ed's silence was all the confirmation Caesar needed. He took in the anger spreading across their faces, but nothing compared to the rage welling up in his chest.

"Yes, Niles, these two slimy motherfuckas were planning to steal millions from me and snatch the drug game from right underneath my feet. Isn't that right, fellas?"

"We wouldn't do nothin' like that to our brother!" Joseph jumped to his feet and balled his fists.

"Still putting up the act, I see. But let me tell you what I know so you can cut the shit. The morning he was murdered, my dad made mention of business that he had to handle. I put two and two together and figured he was planning to meet with Damián Alverez. So I put a call into him myself, and guess what he told me?"

"What?" Joseph humored him through clenched teeth.

"He told me that in fact he did have a meeting with my dad. The only thing was, he never showed. And later Damián found out he'd been killed."

"He's lying. He killed Cassius!"

"That was something that ran across my mind, but I just couldn't shake the feeling that something more was at play. I couldn't stop thinking that the men who swore their lives to protect my dad didn't have one single bullet hole in them, yet my father had ten. I had forensics run a few of the shells found at the scene, and guess what? They were a match for the exact kind used for a handgun purchased in Ed's name earlier this year."

"Caes, what are you sayin'?" Niles asked slowly.

"You know what I'm saying," Caesar said and turned back to the other two. "I'm going to ask you both again, when did you two and my father stop being friends? Why did you kill him?"

A chill came across the room, and it was taking everything in Caesar to stay seated behind the desk. Both Ed and Joseph were frozen in place, seemingly trying to find their words. Finally, Ed gave up attempting to search for a lie in his brain. In the end, he just shrugged his broad shoulders carelessly and smirked.

"I stopped being Cassius's friend a long time ago. I mean, you really can't be friends with your boss, can you?"

"So you killed him?"

"We did. Cassius was a madman, talking crazy ideas. What he proposed would have caused more bloodshed. When we got the chance to knock him off the chessboard, we took the opportunity. When you think about it, we saved many lives by taking one."

"Don't try to make what you did sound all noble. You killed him out of greed, nothing else."

"Oh, my God, Ed! Can we stop talkin' to this jive nigga and just kill him? We got shit to do!" Joseph exclaimed, whipping out his pistol.

"You should have just taken our offer." Ed shook his head and stood up.

Caesar didn't notice the gun in Ed's hand until it was pointed at his face. Niles tried to go for his own weapon, but Joseph had his on him before it could happen. If looks could kill, the hate in Caesar's eyes surely would have surely murdered them.

"You killed a great man, do you know that? Your greed led you to make the worst mistake of your life."

"From where I'm standing, it feels like the best one I've made." Ed smiled big and showcased the gap between his two front teeth. "All this time bein' Cassius's sidekick, I think I'm due for a reward or two. You bein' out of the way is just the icin' on the cake. And don't worry, we'll find the new safe houses, get the money, and continue business as usual. You should have come here with more than this nigga. Maybe you would have stood a chance."

"The first mistake you made today was assuming that I didn't know what you did." Caesar could tell that Ed thought his final speech would have more of an effect on him, but Caesar didn't bat an eye. In fact, he felt no fear in his heart as he spoke. "The second was assuming I didn't figure you would try to kill me once you knew that I found out the truth. So that would make your third mistake assuming that I would ever walk into that without a plan."

"And what plan is that?"

"Him." Caesar nodded his head at someone behind the two of them.

They'd been so high on the thought of their victory that Ed and Joseph hadn't even heard the armed Mexican men enter, Damián Alverez being one of them. He wasted no time in motioning a bored hand toward Ed and Joseph.

"Kill them," he said coldly.

Boom! Boom!

The shots rang out, and the bullets from the guns met their mark. When Joseph's and Ed's bodies fell, Damián stepped over them like they weren't even there. He took a seat on the green sofa, crossing a leg over the other, and faced Boogie.

"All right. Let's get down to business, shall we?"

Even if it is unpleasant, always play your position.

Chapter 13

"Well, my question has been answered before it had to leave my mouth," Damián said as the two men he'd brought with him stood like the royal guards in England on either side of the couch. Their eyes were locked in on Caesar, watching his every move.

Niles stood firmly beside Caesar, that time with his gun drawn. He didn't want to take another chance of not being prepared in the face of danger. It also didn't help that the newcomers didn't look very friendly.

"And what question would that be?"

"I thought the reason you wanted to meet was to see if I had something to do with Cassius's murder. But we both know the truth now. I heard everything." Damián glanced down at the dead bodies.

"And I'll be the first to say that I'm glad about it. Because it makes this next step easy. Do you know why my father wanted to meet with you, Damián?"

"I could guess, but I would rather not waste time. Tell me."

"He wanted your territory. You would still have a part to play, of course. But he wanted to turn a king into a prince."

"I see."

"After he got you where he wanted you, he would go to the next family, and the next. Until he was the most powerful man in New York City."

"And you called me here because you want to finish what he started, I suppose?"

"On the contrary actually. I think it's time to put the old deck of cards away and shuffle some new ones. We've seen how much of a muck we create when we are all divided. Why not see what we can create together?"

"And why should I join forces with a *boy* like you?"

"Because it's no secret that I'm now head of the strongest family of the five. We might not be able to win against you all at once, but we can damn sure mop the floor with the Alverez family. We've done it before. Do I need to remind you of what happened in the summer of '74? I was fourteen and on the front line for that. You've seen firsthand what this 'boy' can do."

At the mention of the massacre that had taken place four years prior, Damián cleared his throat uncomfortably. Everything Caesar spoke was true. Damián and Caesar had a disagreement about who could do what where, and it enraged Cassius so bad that every time someone in Damián's camp was seen that summer, they had to die. Caesar had a lot of blood on his hands from it.

"And that is one very big reason why my people will never accept this."

"In the art of war, war should be avoided with diplomacy at all costs. The feuding between us has been the first resort when really it should have been the last. Your people only have to accept whatever you do. Especially with what I can do for you."

"I've already done a favor for you. Two actually." Damián pointed at Ed and Joseph.

"While I am appreciative of that, it's nothing compared to what I'm bringing to the table."

"And that is?"

"For starters, I know that your side of the fence has recently had a run-in with the law. I also know that there's a good chance you might go down this time."

"So you're telling me you can make all of it go away?"

"Now that would take a miracle. Somebody will definitely have to do some time. But I *am* saying I can get their eyes off you."

"You working with them?"

"I might have a mole or two who can get you out of a sticky situation. But I'm going to need something from you in return." Caesar watched as the wheels in Damián's head turned.

"Name your price," he finally said.

"I understand that you and the Chinese are in good standing."

"I guess you can say that."

"Good. I need you to convince Wang Lei to have a sit-down meeting with me alongside Benjamin and Domino."

"Are you certain you can make such a meeting happen?"

"Domino for sure will be there. The Dominicans have fought the least. But Benjamin might take some wearing down. I'm sure he can be convinced though."

"Okay. If you keep your end of the bargain, I will do this favor for you."

"Then we'll be in touch."

Caesar stood up and shook Damián's hand before he left with his men. Caesar stepped around the desk and turned his nose up at the dead bodies. Most people would have wanted to kill their loved one's killers themselves, but it didn't matter to Caesar, because their deaths weren't enough. Tormenting them for days wouldn't have been enough. Nothing would change the fact that his life had been altered forever. All he could do was push forward, and the next call to action was an easy one.

"Niles—"

"I already know. Whoever these motherfuckas were close to have to go. I'll handle it."

"Thanks. I just can't take any risk right now."

"Understood. I'm about to pull the car to the alley so we can dump the bodies. Grab some plastic or somethin'."

By the time Caesar dropped Niles off at home and made it to his next destination, he was sure Ed and Joseph had touched the bottom of the Hudson River. He walked through the Museum of Glass and Fine Art not surprised to see that it wasn't very busy at that hour. However, he did spot a man wearing a pair of jeans, a hoodie, and sunglasses sitting on a bench. It looked as if he were looking at the painting in front of him, but Caesar knew better. The man was waiting for someone, and that someone was him. Caesar approached the bench and sat down on the opposite end. No one was around, but still the men didn't look at each other. They both just stared straight ahead.

"Thank you for meeting me here, Detective Easley," Caesar said, breaking the silence.

"Did I have a choice?" the detective asked.

"You always have a choice. You just happened to make the right one."

"Yeah, yeah. Did you get my message about the bullets?"

"I did. And that knowledge came in handy."

"You handled the problem, I assume."

"You know I did."

"Great. Then we have no further business," Easley stated and made to get up.

"Sit down," Caesar instructed. "I wouldn't be here if I didn't need your services anymore. I need you to do something for me."

Easley clenched his jaw tightly and slowly sat back down. The frown on his thin lips told Caesar that he wasn't too happy with the turn of events. One thing that the streets would soon learn about Caesar was that he adapted quickly. Although it pained him deeply to see his father go, he accepted it for what it was. The other thing they would learn was that he was very strategic. He knew there would be hands out for his throne, which was why he jumped into action the same day he learned his father had died. Cassius would have wanted his son to mourn him, but he would want him to secure the empire more. And that was exactly what he had done.

The first thing he did was make sure the police who were in his father's pocket hopped into his. But he was going to go a step further. He was going to pocket a Fed, too, and he knew just the one. With one phone call he was able to get the tapes of the recorded conversations between himself and Gerald. Once they were in his possession, he was also able to get Easley's address to plant them and take photos. Between the photos and surveillance of him entering the King residence, Caesar had more than enough to blackmail Easley as the one who tampered with the evidence of a drug bust.

"I didn't become a detective to take orders from someone like you," Easley sneered.

"Then don't look at them as orders. Look at them as favors. Favors that come with nice rewards."

Caesar reached inside his jacket pocket and pulled out an envelope containing $5,000. He gave it to Easley, who opened it and quickly shut it again. He glanced around to make sure nobody had seen the exchange and finally turned to face Caesar.

"I can't take this much money. I won't even be able to spend it!"

"You will if you clean it. Take whatever money you have already saved up and open up an ice cream shop here in Manhattan. Don't worry about what you're spending. You'll make it back in no time as long as you do what I need you to do."

Easley looked at the envelope in his hands and seemed to ponder his options. Finally, he came to a choice, and again, he made the decision that pleased Caesar. He tucked the envelope inside his own jacket pocket.

"What do you need me to do?"

"Whatever evidence they have on Damián Alverez? I need it destroyed."

"What? I can't do that. It's the biggest bust in the department so far this year!"

"You can and you will. Otherwise, you'll be too busy getting arrested to enjoy that bust. The evidence needs to be nonexistent and not hidden like the tapes were. Pin the bust on one of the men you have in custody. That way you still get your bust."

"And what do you get?"

"Hopefully unity."

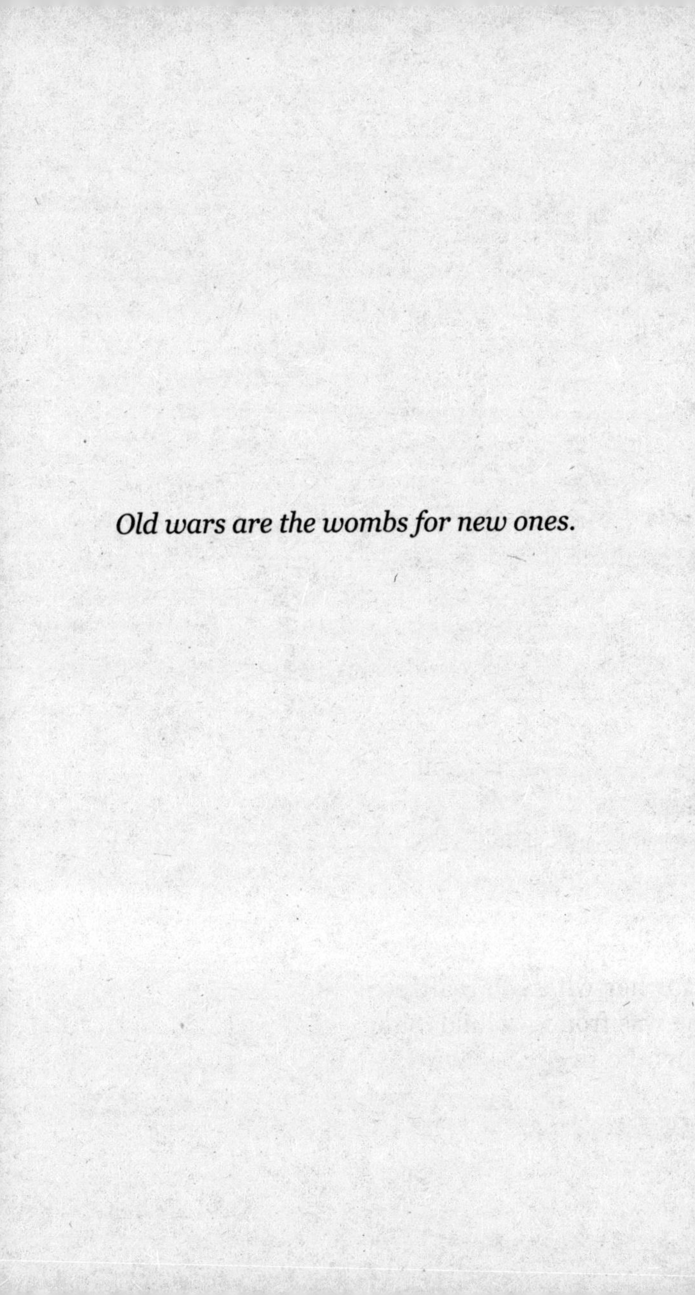

Old wars are the wombs for new ones.

Chapter 14

The Present

Caesar stopped talking, and Boogie sat up in his bed. He had an eager look on his face, but what Caesar paid attention to was the drooping of his eyes. He needed rest.

"That's it? You're just gon' stop the story there?"

"I'll tell you the rest another time. You need to rest."

"Like I said before, I'll rest when I'm dead," Boogie said, leaning back into his pillow. "Wow . . . Marco's old man was a gangster. He came in and just popped them two niggas like that? And Niles! Is he—"

"Nathan and Nicky's father? Yes," Caesar said fondly, thinking of his cousin. "He was my cousin but also my closest friend. I have never known a loyalty like his. When I lost him, everyone thought I took his boys in because it was my duty, and I guess they were right in a way. But you know why I really did it?"

"Love?"

"Of course. But even more so because I could feel his spirit living on through them. Them being in my life helped me not feel his loss."

"Damn, Caesar, I'm just now realizing how many of your people have died."

Boogie's words resonated deeply within Caesar. It was true. Over the years he had lost count of how many of his loved ones had been lost to the game. Some of them died protecting him. But no matter how many people were lost, a person never got used to saying goodbye, especially when it happened out of nowhere. He smiled sadly.

"It comes with the territory. I'm hoping you break that curse."

"Well, I'm off to a pretty bad start." Boogie shook his head. "I'm so mad at myself about this mess. I should have killed that motherfucka when I had the chance."

"Why didn't you?" Caesar asked, and Boogie mulled over the question for a few moments.

"Because of Amber, I guess. I didn't know if I would be able to look her in the eyes when she was older, knowing that I killed her biological dad."

"And how do you feel about it now?"

"That nigga shot me! He gotta die!" Boogie exclaimed. "I'm a man down right now because of him. I can't even get out there to look for my baby girl. I'm useless."

"You could never be useless."

"I am though. Tazz and them are doin' the best they can to keep everything in my camp in order. There are a lot of jobs on the table, and I'm just hopin' they can sort them all out."

"Tazz has been in the game for a while. He's a hard worker and he's loyal. You don't have anything to worry about."

"I just hate this shit."

"I would rather you be bedridden than in a coffin," Caesar told him. "Before I leave, I just want to say that I know things have been hard on you since Barry died. Maneuvering through a world like this one without the person who taught you everything you need to know about it has to be hard. But I for one am proud of you."

"Caesar, you don't have to say all this," Boogie said, blinking the water away from his eyes.

"I know I don't have to say it, but I want to. It's long overdue. There aren't many men who can stand what you have and run an empire effortlessly. And if I'm proud of you, then I know for a fact Barry is."

"I hope so." Boogie nodded and wiped his tears away with the palm of his hand.

"I know so. What doesn't kill you only makes you stronger, and the pain you're experiencing right now is turning you into a titan. And to double back on what you said, we're going to bring Amber home."

"I know . . . I know Bentley won't let me down. He never has before."

"Keep that faith. Remember that manifestation is just a strong belief in something."

Caesar started to get up, but Boogie stopped him. "Wait. Before you go, I have one more question," he said. "Detective Easley—he still around?"

"Yes, he's around but retired. However, he still works at his beloved ice cream shop," Caesar said. "His son followed in his footsteps and became a Fed. Luckily for all of us, he did it for the right *and* wrong reasons."

"So he works for you?"

"For us."

At that moment Boogie gave a big yawn, and Caesar knew it was time to take his leave. Even if the boy wanted to keep talking, sleep was winning the battle. His eyes shut and didn't open again, but a small snore escaped his lips. Caesar patted Boogie's hand twice in farewell and left the bedroom. Now that he knew Boogie was okay, it was time to shift his focus to Louisa.

Lorenzo Alverez felt like he was going to explode if he saw one more bouquet of flowers. The entire living room of his family home was filled with them. Different kinds and colors just everywhere, reminding him of what had been lost. No, of what had been taken. The death of his sister Daniella so soon after his father was too much of a blow. So much in fact that Christina, Zo's mother, decided not to have a traditional funeral. It had been very fast and intimate, and the family who was not in attendance sent their condolences with cards or flowers to the house. Laying Daniella to rest might have been quick, but the mourning process had just begun.

Daniella had been Zo's first friend. They bumped heads like any normal brother and sister, but the love between them was true. He wished that things toward the end could have been different. But their father's death had driven an invisible wedge between them. She felt that their father built his empire solely for him to rule one day. She didn't feel that she had a rightful place. The anger she felt from that clouded her judgment when it came to Louisa. Their aunt had fed into Daniella's desire for power and tricked her into believing that she would have them. She tricked her all the way up until she pulled the trigger.

Both Zo and his mother were taking the losses hard, but Christina had become a shell of her former self. She hadn't eaten or gotten a good night's sleep since she saw Daniella in a pool of her own brains and blood. All she wanted to do was be alone, so much so that she temporarily relieved all the hired help. Zo didn't want to leave her alone.

He wanted to say it was solely to comfort her, but another reason was because he didn't know the true depths of her despair. She hadn't given any signs of self-harm, but there was a big difference between having a broken heart and it being ripped out of one's chest. The truth was he didn't know what she would do.

The two of them were sitting in the kitchen, and he was trying to get her to drink something. She was pale in the face, and her long, beautiful hair was disheveled. Her eyes were open but didn't seem to see anything, and she barely spoke more than five sentences a day.

"*Mamá,* you have to eat something," Zo said, holding a piece of a sandwich up to her lips, but she turned her head away.

"I'm not hungry," she said.

"You haven't eaten anything in days. Please, just one bite."

"I . . . I can't." She shook her head. "I just can't, Lorenzo. Please leave me alone."

"I can't do that, *Mamá*. I won't do that."

"Why won't everyone just leave me be? I don't need anyone to check on me and remind me . . . remind me that they're gone. Stop asking if I'm okay or trying to get me to eat. I can't! I *can't.*"

"We're all we have left. We have to look out for each other." Lorenzo took her hands in his and kissed them.

His words made tears come to her eyes. She took in a quick breath like she was trying to stop a sob from coming out. He'd never seen her look so defeated before. Her hands trembled in his, and Zo felt a strong surge of love for her. He understood why she'd sent everyone away. She was one who needed strength, not pity. She didn't need anyone to patch up her wounds. She needed someone to remind her there was still something to live for.

"Why did she go with that evil woman? Why did she trust her?"

"Daniella felt . . . I don't know. I think she wanted to be seen."

"But I *saw* her. I loved her."

"I know you did, *Mamá*. This isn't on you. If anything, this is on me."

"No! This is on Louisa. She preyed on you both, and she killed my baby. I need you to promise me something."

"Anything."

"When you kill that bitch, don't make it quick."

Christina's eyes pierced his, and he nodded his head. He already had plans on bleeding Louisa dry, but now he was even more motivated to do so. He wasn't just carrying his pain anymore. He was carrying his mother's as well.

Ding-dong!

The loud ringing of the doorbell filled the entire home, and Zo knew he would have to be the one to answer it. He got up and went to the front door. When he opened it, he expected it to be another bouquet of flowers since the men watching the gate were only letting mail through. And he was right. In front of him was a deliveryman holding a dozen roses inside of a crystal vase. The only difference between those flowers and the rest was that the others were colorful. These roses were black as death.

"Just sign right here and I'll be on my way," the older deliveryman said, handing Zo a small clipboard.

Zo signed on the line and took the flowers inside. He watched the deliveryman get back in his truck and pull off before shutting the door again. Zo walked to the living room to place the flowers with the rest, but he noticed that there was a small note card attached to one of the stems.

Sunday evening at eight o'clock. The Blues fishing dock.

The note was signed with the letter L, and he knew the L was for Louisa. Zo instantly saw red. He threw the vase across the room, and it shattered against the wall, sending glass everywhere.

"Lorenzo! What is it?" Christina shouted and rushed to the living room.

There was a look of pure rage on his face. He turned to her frightened face and crumpled the note in his hand. He let out a breath like a brazen bull and flexed his muscles, envisioning everything he was going to do to Louisa.

"Lorenzo?" Christina asked again and pried the note from his hands. She read it and clenched her jaw. "She's trying to kill you too."

"No . . . she still wants me. She wants to have me around her finger like she had *Papá*."

"Over my dead body!"

"The only dead body will be hers. I'm tripling security around the house. And I'm calling the help and telling them all to come back tomorrow."

"Lorenzo—"

"*Mamá,* you don't heal by running away from your life. You heal by continuing to live it. And I need to make sure you're not alone while I'm gone."

"I don't need anyone to—"

"It's not up for debate. I'm asking you to respect me the way you did *Papá*. And I'm only asking before I have to tell you. The roles have switched. You already took care of me. It's my turn to take care of you. I'm calling Rosaline to come now."

He realized he would have to put his mourning for Daniella on pause. There was another war at his feet. And that one had his name written all over it.

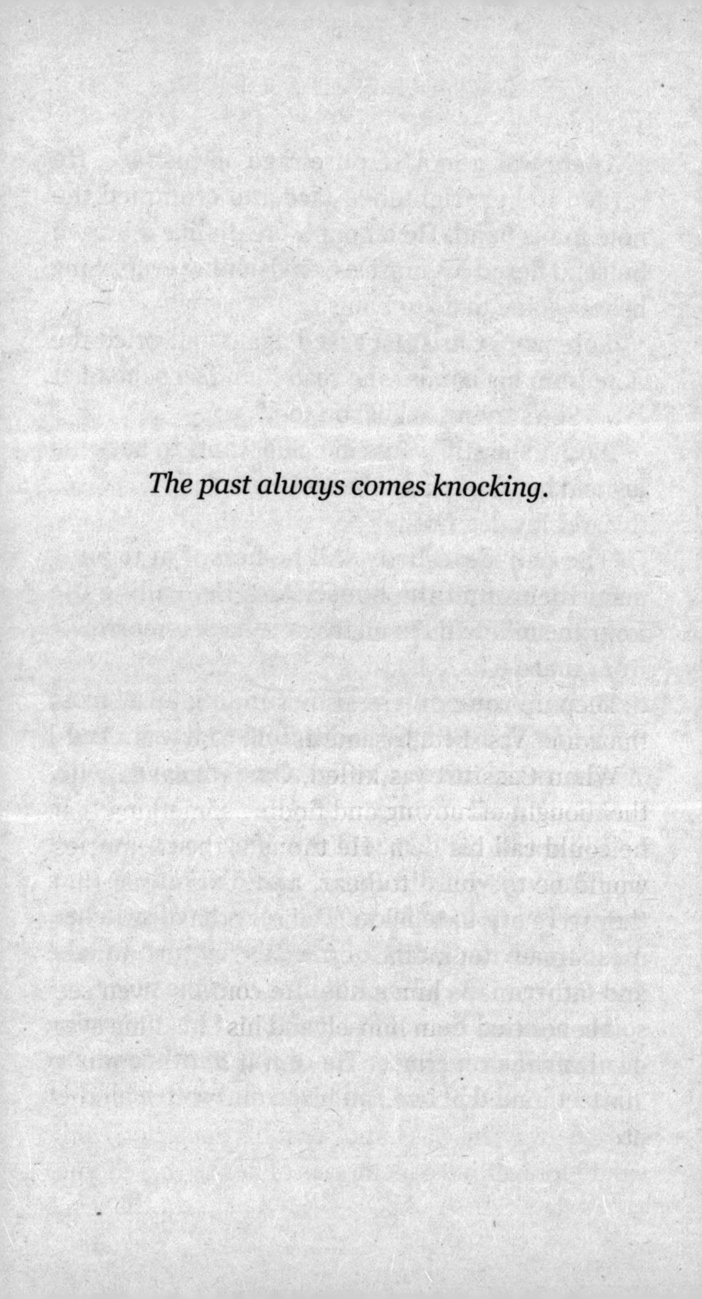

The past always comes knocking.

Chapter 15

It wasn't until Caesar arrived at his home that he felt just how truly exhausted he was. It wasn't even five o'clock yet, but his bed was calling his name. He stepped inside the mansion, as he had done many times before, but that time he stopped in the foyer to survey the home. Well, what he could see from there. There had been many upgrades done to keep up with the times, but the foundation of the home was still the same as when he was a boy.

When Cassius was killed, Caesar played with the thought of moving and finding something that he could call his own. He thought the memories would be too hard to bear, and it was true that they were a tough pill to swallow sometimes. But most times the memories he had of his mother and father made him smile. He couldn't even see someone other than himself and his bloodline ever owning the property, so he kept it and eventually started his own family there. And when Amira passed away, he was happy that his daughter, Milli, would forever have memories of her in their home.

"Daddy, is that you?" Milli's voice called before she appeared at the top of the stairs. She was dressed in lounge clothes and had a messy bun on top of her head. He hadn't seen her look so comfortable since she was a teenager. Now it was usually business attire or nightlife wear.

When she saw that it was in fact him, she smiled from ear to ear and bounded down the steps. He opened his arms just in time for her to fly into them. It felt good to hug his baby girl after weeks of being apart.

"Hey, baby girl," Caesar said and kissed her forehead.

"I was hoping it was you when I saw the car pull up!" Milli pulled away from him, still beaming. "But I thought you would be gone for at least another month!"

"I thought so too, but some things came up."

"Things like what?"

"Nothing you need to worry your head with," he assured her. "How have things been here?"

"Surprisingly quiet. Nicky and Nathan come over and check on me when they can, but that's about it."

"Are you doing all right?"

"Yes, even though I missed you terribly! You hungry? Come eat something! You look tired."

She took him into the kitchen and made him sit down at the table while she fixed him something quick to eat. While she was doing so, Caesar noticed that it was very quiet around the house. In fact, he hadn't seen his gardener outside watering the plants, nor had he been greeted by the help when he walked through the front door.

"Where is everyone at?"

"Everyone like who?" Milli asked, setting a plate in front of him and pouring a glass of ice water.

"The people I pay to keep up this place."

"Oh, them. I gave them the week off."

"You what? Milli, don't tell me you've been in this house alone for a week."

"Daddy, they work so hard! I just wanted to do something nice for them. And I mean, I thought I would be fine. Security is still outside, so I was all good."

"That's not the point. I don't like the idea of you being inside alone."

"Well, if it makes you feel any better, I've slept with a .40 tucked under my pillow every night."

"That actually does make me feel a little bit better. But I'm making sure everyone reports for their regular shifts tomorrow."

"Fine by me." She took a seat at the table and propped her chin on her hand. "Sooo . . . how was your vacay with Auntie Diana?"

"While it lasted it was nice."

"Did you meet anybody while you were down there?" Milli asked, trying to mask the hopeful tinge to her tone.

"Here you go with this."

"What? I just don't want you to grow old alone. I guess I should say *older*."

"Watch yourself now," Caesar laughed and took a bite of the pasta Milli had warmed up for him.

"I'm just saying! I don't remember the last time I saw you date someone. You're a handsome guy. There are tons of women out there who would love to be on the arm of Caesar King."

"Just because you didn't see it doesn't mean it didn't happen. I've had my fair share of women over the past few years, but nobody as noteworthy as your mother."

"Let you tell it, nobody will ever be either. Mom has been gone for years now. Don't you think it's time to move on? I mean, I loved her as much as you do, but I'm sure she wouldn't want you to be alone."

It wasn't the first time Milli had tried to talk Caesar into finding love again. He knew her heart was in the right place, but she didn't understand the first thing about Caesar's heart and loyalty. It transcended time and space. Life and death. He thought of her mother's smile and felt a warmness in his chest.

"I'll tell you something, Milli. Sometimes in life you just meet that one person who sends your world upside down in the most wonderful way. And most times you only meet that person once.

And your mother was that for me. Amira wasn't just the love of my life. She was my soul mate. And although I may share my bed with another woman from time to time, my heart will never be at anyone else's disposal. I'm okay with that."

"Fine," Milli grumbled. "I guess I'll do away with my dreams of planning the perfect wedding for you."

"Save that energy for your own love life, my dear."

"I wouldn't hold your breath. Plus, the only man I'm remotely interested in is . . . far away."

Caesar's interest was piqued. He'd never heard her mention any love interest before. She always seemed to be so busy in her studies to date. But before he could ask for any details on her mystery man, the doorbell rang, and she got up to answer it.

"I'll get it!"

"Yeah, you better, since you sent everybody home."

She grinned at him and left to answer the door. A few minutes later she returned to the kitchen, but she wasn't alone. In tow was a handsome young white man with familiar blond hair and blue eyes. The badge around his neck spoke loudly of who and what he was.

"You have a visitor, Daddy."

"I guess I do. Milli, why don't you go upstairs to your suite and let me and the detective talk?"

"Okay. Call me if you need me."

She left, and Caesar offered his guest a seat at the table. The detective sat in the seat Milli had just occupied and scooted up to the table.

"It's been a while since I had to make a house call, Caesar, so I apologize for showing up unannounced."

"Don't apologize. Especially when house calls were your father's favorite thing to do," Caesar said with a smile. "How is the old man anyway?"

Detective Michael Easley was the son of Jacob Easley. When Michael came of age, he followed right in his father's footsteps. And when Jacob retired from the force, he passed the torch to his son. From then on out, he was the one who reported to Caesar and kept the Feds off his six. And in return, Caesar made sure he had everything his heart desired.

"Cancer is kicking his ass," Michael answered. "He doesn't have much longer."

"I'm sorry to hear that, son," Caesar told him, genuinely saddened by the news. "I'll have to go and see him. You may not know, but your old man and I didn't start off on the right foot. But after all these years, I can truly say that he has been one of my greatest friends."

"I don't know much about the beginning, but I know that now he would walk through fire for you. All these years you looked out for each other."

"And now I can do the same for you. Just let me know when you're ready for a promotion. The captain frequents the Sugar Trap, and from what Diana tells me, that motherfucka has a lot of kink in him. Just say the word."

Caesar expected Michael to laugh, but he didn't. He didn't even crack a smile, and that was when he knew something wasn't right.

"Thank you, Caesar, really, but that can wait. I'm just here to talk to you about your boy."

"My boy?"

"Yeah, Boogie. I don't know the specifics, but when they brought him into the hospital, I knew it wasn't a safe place for him."

"You're the one who switched the bodies."

"I did. It just so happens that at the same time Boogie was shot, I had to kill a damn drug fiend for trying to attack me in that alley behind Joe's Donuts. Crazy motherfucker, too. Anyways, one of my guys is a surgeon at the hospital Boogie was being taken to. After he performed the surgery, we swapped the bodies and said Boogie was a DOA."

"So how do we smooth all of this over when it's found out he's not dead?"

"Just have him lie low for a while, and then we tell the world it was a case of mistaken identity. Believe it or not, it happens all the time. Hell, it happened with you. Nicky might be questioned, but he can just say he was so fucked up by grief that he wasn't seeing straight that day."

"Hmm," Caesar found himself chuckling. "You might be better at this than your father was."

"Don't let him hear you say that," Michael said and smiled. "I want him to go knowing that he was the best good criminal there was."

"Ha! Trust me, I won't say a thing. Wait here for a minute." Caesar got up from the table.

He left and came back a few moments later holding a small duffle bag. Michael caught it when Caesar tossed it to him and unzipped it. Twenty thousand dollars' worth of Benjamin Franklins stared up at him, and his smile turned into a grin.

"Pleasure doing business with you."

"Make sure you break your guy off something, too, for patching Boogie up."

"Of course," Michael said and zipped the bag back up. "And, Caesar, there's one more reason why I stopped by today."

"Something wrong?"

"I don't know." Michael made a face. "You know what's been going on on Staten Island?"

"Boogie has been handling things over that way. I'm sure he's going to have Bentley overseeing things while he is out of commission."

"And the Italians have been okay with this hostile takeover since Bosco died?"

"I've heard there have been some problems, but Boogie has them under control."

"Maybe for now, but . . ."

"But what?"

"My dad told me the stories. That the Italians might have been the face of business there, but someone else was really running the show. And with that being said, you don't think it's been quiet since Bosco died? I mean *too* quiet."

"If you mean what I think you mean, in order to get to Boogie, he'll have to go through me. And he hasn't shown his face in years."

"I hear you. But I think what Boogie did might bring him out of the shadows. My dad told me the stories, and all I'm going to say is be careful."

"And as always, I appreciate the words of advice."

Michael got up from the table and tossed the bag over his shoulder. Caesar shook his hand before walking him out. When Caesar shut the door, he was left to the silence of his own home. It made him think about what Michael had just said. In all the havoc of recent events, there was one issue that he hadn't thought of. It hadn't made its way to his front door yet, but when it did, he would address it the way he should have a long time ago.

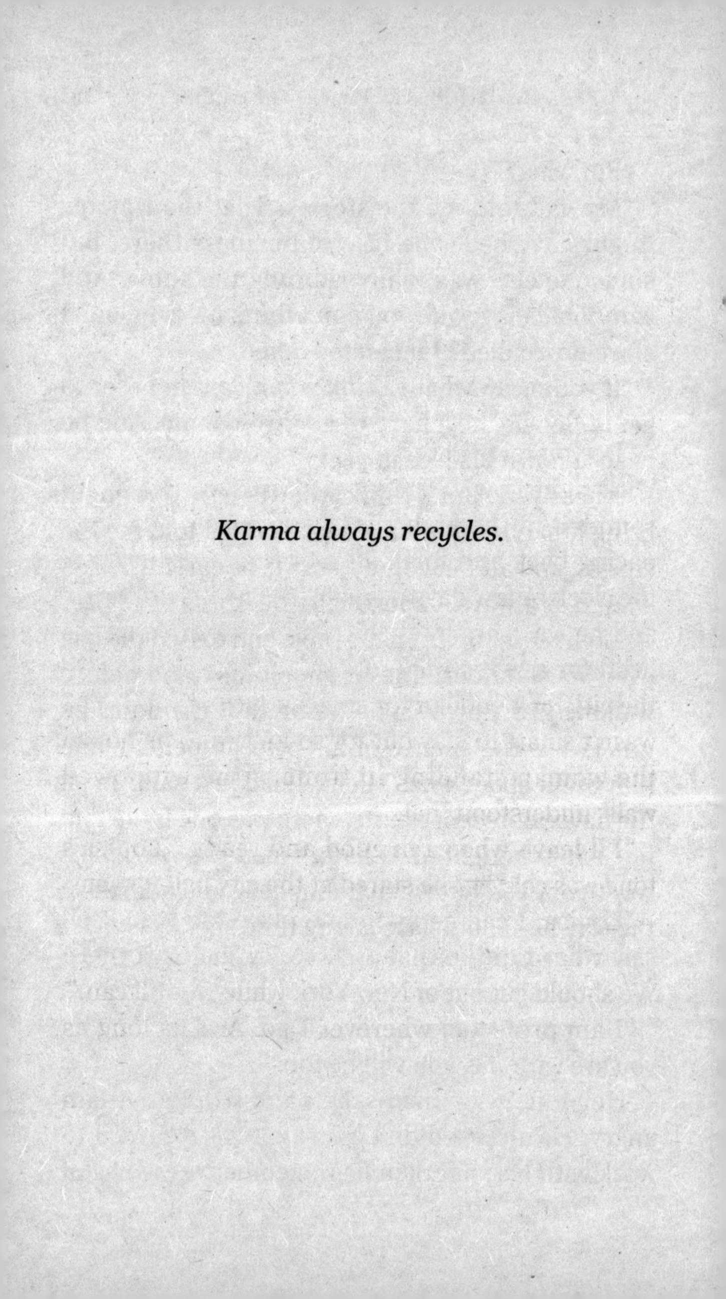

Karma always recycles.

Chapter 16

"Do you really think it's a good idea to be in New York right now?" The voice of Adam McGregory sounded in the high-rise hotel suite. He'd been pacing back and forth all morning and checking the clock. A few days passed since he killed Boogie, and he was sure by then there was a price on his head for a hefty amount. He didn't want to be in the city long enough for someone to collect. It just wasn't smart to stay out for so long, and he hoped the woman standing in front of the windowed walls understood that.

"I'll leave when I'm good and ready." Louisa's tone was cold as she stared at the city below them.

"Louisa, I can't stay in one place too long. You saw what I did to that asshole Boogie back there. We should get out of New York while we still can."

"I am protected wherever I go. And as long as you are with me, you will be too."

Her tone was dismissive, and it made Adam angry. He almost didn't know why he'd agreed to work with her, but then he remembered the bag of money. And his rage didn't help. He was so mad at Boogie that he would do anything to get back at him. That blind rage seemed to lead him down a street with no outlet. He hadn't thought about the ricochet effect of his actions. And at that point, Louisa was making him feel unheard.

"You think you can go against four families and come out untouched?" Adam scoffed. "If you do, then you really haven't thought this through. It isn't like before when you could move in the shadows because nobody saw you coming. They know you're here, and you have blood on your hands just like I have on mine!"

"I don't need you to remind me what I have done. I have no regrets." Louisa turned away from the window and faced Adam. Her eyes shot daggers at him. "Are you afraid?"

"I'm not scared of shit. But I'd be a fool to think there isn't a price on my head."

"And it doesn't help that you took that baby, correct?"

They both looked over at Adam's daughter, Amber, who was on the floor playing with some toys. He bought them for her when he realized just how disconnected he was from his child. She wouldn't stop crying when he first took her. He hated Roz and Boogie even more for that. He'd been robbed of fatherhood without his consent. Amber still was hesitant with him because she didn't know him, but with time Adam thought that maybe it would get better. She was his, and he made the decision that he would raise her, or try to. He couldn't think of a better way to hurt Roz than to take the two things she loved most in the world.

"She's my daughter."

"And a reason why the price on your head is most likely doubled. They probably have a twenty-four-hour watch for you all around the city." Louisa walked toward him, her heels clicking on the marble floors beneath them, until she was just inches away. "You should watch how you speak to me. Be pleased that I personally haven't killed you for becoming so much of a liability. I have chosen to give you grace."

"Grace?" Adam asked incredulously. "Is that what you call this? Matter of fact, I have a better question. If I'm such a liability, why spare me in the first place?"

"Because I still need you."

"For what?"

"Every villain needs a sidekick." Louisa's lips curled slightly.

"Yeah, well, you murdered her, didn't you?"

"My niece didn't have the gumption to do what you did. In the beginning, I thought she was strong, but in the end, I realized she was a weak little girl wanting to cling to something. I'd grown fond of her, yes. But there is no place in this business for someone like that. Someone so . . . needy. But you? When I saw you shoot Boogie, I knew you could be an asset to me. But now, I'm not so sure. You're acting like a scared pussycat."

"Listen, I've never been a pussy. Prison just made me cautious. And it's not rocket science to see that doing what I did has major consequences. Now that I'm responsible for Amber, I'm not staying here."

"What exactly are you saying, Adam?"

"I'm saying I've done everything you asked me to do. That was all I agreed to. So you can find yourself another damn sidekick, because it won't be me. I'ma take the money you paid me and get out of town. Now if you'll excuse me, I'll be on my way."

Louisa lifted a brow, and her right hand twitched slightly, almost like she wanted to slap him. Adam watched her fight her urges to punish him for speaking to her in such a tone, but eventually she took a deep breath. When she exhaled, her tight face loosened up, and her shoulders relaxed.

"Are you sure you want to leave my protection?"

"Is this protection, or just another prison? Because it feels like the second choice to me," Adam growled.

"That's where you're wrong. You can't leave a prison," she said and stepped out of his way. "But here, you're free to go."

Adam didn't hesitate to make his move. He scooped Amber up into his arms, and surprisingly, she didn't make a fuss. She seemed to be ready to go too. He grabbed a few of the toys, and with one last look at Louisa, he went to the suite's door. Louisa's guards didn't budge from where they stood in front of it and prevented him from exiting.

"He can pass," Louisa told them.

Slowly they stepped out of the way and let him leave. When the door closed, Louisa shrugged her shoulders. Both guards had flabbergasted expressions on their faces.

"You're just going to let him go like that?" one of them asked. "I hoped you would give us the order to kill him for the way he was talking to you."

"Yes, I'm going to let him go," Louisa answered and went back to looking out the window. She smirked down at the street. "Trust me, what's waiting for him is much worse than anything I could ever do."

Amber fussed in Adam's arms on the way out of the hotel, so much so that he received many curious stares from people passing by. Trying to give the illusion of a loving dad, he tried to laugh it off and kiss her on the forehead, but that only made her more volatile.

"It's okay, Amber, it's okay." Adam patted her back and bounced her on his hip.

He hurried to get to where his car was parked in the public garage. As he walked, he kept checking over his shoulder. He couldn't shake the feeling that he was being followed or watched. Louisa had let him go easily, but he wondered if she would change her mind. Just in case, Adam wanted to be far away from her if she did.

Once he got to the car, he rushed to strap Amber safely in her car seat. However, she didn't make it very easy. Her arms flailed everywhere, and she kicked her feet. If Adam got a strap over her shoulder, she would just pull her arm free again.

"Amber, stop!" he shouted, terrifying the child.

Tears welled in her eyes, and she began to holler loudly. In a split second a switch flipped in his head. Taking her away from Roz had been a knee-jerk reaction to the disrespect Adam had felt. He'd been so angry with her for not letting him be a father to Amber that he never truly asked himself if he really wanted to be. He looked down at the baby's scrunched-up and tearful face and felt . . . nothing. There was no connection. He didn't know her and . . . he really didn't like her. Who was he kidding? He wanted her for one reason and one reason only: because Roz did.

Adam finally had his freedom and enough money to last him a long time, and he wanted to make up for the time he had lost. And a kid didn't really fit into the lifestyle he truly wanted. But still, even with that revelation, he didn't want Roz to have her. Adam wanted her to be in pain every second of every hour from then on out. And there was only one other way to make that happen. He glanced at the floor of the back of the car and saw a sweatshirt lying there.

"Ahhh! Ahhh!" Amber's cries continued to echo in the garage.

Adam just wanted it to stop. He just wanted her to be quiet, and she had no intention of doing so. She was crying so hard that she was sweating, and her face was starting to turn red. He grabbed the sweatshirt and balled it up in his hands.

"Shut up. Just shut up!" Adam shouted.

But she didn't. The stream of tears falling down her face only got thicker and her cries louder. He had to make it stop. Adam went to place the balled shirt over her face, coming to terms with the fact that he was about to end his own child's life.

"I wouldn't do that if I were you," a sudden voice behind him warned.

It was menacing and followed by the sound of a gun cocking. Adam froze with the shirt centimeters from Amber's face. He dropped it and put his palms out as if to say he wasn't armed.

"She said she was going to let me go," he said.

"She did. I didn't."

"And who are you?"

"Turn around and see."

Slowly, Adam did what he was told. The man pulled down the hood that was over his head, revealing his identity. In the heat of the moment, Adam didn't recognize him at first. But then his memory came back to him.

"Bentley," he said, looking into the face of Roz's brother.

"I know you weren't about to do what I think you were about to do to my niece, were you?" Bentley's eyes were glacier cold as he stared into Adam's.

There was no right answer. If he said no, Bentley would know he was lying. But if he said yes, Adam was sure he would pull the trigger. So he did the smart thing—he didn't say anything.

"Aw, now you can't speak."

"How did you find me?" Adam asked.

"I'm good at huntin' prey, I guess. I've been waitin' across the street for days for you to leave your room. A couple dollars was all it took for the ladies at the front desk to keep an eye out for you."

"Smart. I guess there isn't a need for me to let my mind wander about why you're here. You want to avenge your fallen friend. The one I put on a T-shirt."

"I'm actually just here to get my niece. And I hate to be the one to break it to you, but you ain't put nobody on a T-shirt. Boogie didn't die."

Adam was tongue-tied. Many things were going through his head, but not a single word formed.

Boogie was alive? Adam thought back to the day he shot him. He'd seen Boogie on the ground bleeding, but in all honesty, he hadn't seen life completely leave him. He'd run before that. Still, Adam was sure he was hurt bad, hence his henchman there with the gun pointed.

"Well, you didn't come here for nothing. Do it," Adam taunted him and stepped forward so the gun was pressed against his forehead.

He watched the man apply pressure to the trigger of the Glock 19 and closed his eyes. Preparing to meet his Maker, Adam took one last breath before it was all over. However, that moment never came. Reopening his eyes, he saw the man lower the gun.

"As much as I want to kill you right now, I won't. There's shit that can be done to you that's a lot worse than death."

On his last word, he hit Adam in the temple with the butt of the gun, knocking him out cold.

There is nothing like a mother scorned.

Chapter 17

Bentley turned up the long drive that led to the tall brick mansion. His car was recognized, so the gate surrounding the property was open before he got to it. He listened to Amber's low snores in the back seat and felt a rush of emotions overcome him. She would never know what kind of danger she had been in. To her, the events probably felt like a dream. Or like a blip in time to her baby mind.

Bentley was grateful that he'd gotten to her just in time. He didn't know what kind of sick man would attempt to kill his own child, a baby at that. It had taken everything in him not to end Adam right then and there, but Bentley knew he wasn't his kill. He was Boogie's. After he was parked in the circular driveway in front of the mansion, he honked his horn to announce his presence. He got out and walked around the car when he saw Roz exit the home. She looked exhausted as she bounded down the stairs wrapped in a long blue kimono.

"Bentley!" She hugged him tightly when she reached him. "I've been trying to call you since yesterday."

"You know I've been out there lookin' for my niece nonstop."

"I know and I appreciate it," she said, stepping back. "I just needed someone here with me, you know? With Boogie down right now, and Amber missing, my mind is just all over the place."

"My bad, sis. You know if I could have been here, I would have been. But Amb bein' out there with that bitch-ass motherfucka had *my* mind goin'. I couldn't come back without her."

"It's okay. I've been praying. I know God is going to bring my baby back. Maybe we should just let the police do their job."

"Police?" Bentley made a face. "We don't need them. Plus, didn't I just say I couldn't come back without her?"

He opened the back door on the right side and revealed a sleeping Amber. Roz gave a gasp of disbelief as she stared at her baby girl safe and sound. Tears fell freely down her cheeks, and her lips quivered when she looked back at her brother. She threw her arms around his neck and squeezed him tighter than before. He hugged her back and wiped his tears away behind her back. When she pulled away from him, Roz didn't waste any time getting Amber out of the car. The beautiful baby girl woke up immediately, almost sensing her mother's presence, and smiled up into Roz's tearful face.

"Oh, Amber. I've missed you so much, baby!" Roz held her close and kissed her all over her little face. "I'll never let anything like that happen to you ever again. I promise. You hear me? I promise!"

Bentley's heart warmed as he watched the mother and daughter being reunited. He'd been relentless about finding Amber and doing it quick. He didn't want to depend on anyone to do it for them. He also couldn't bear the thought of letting his sister and Boogie down. Bentley didn't know Louisa well, but he knew her type—the kind who thought they were invincible. Very high-class and used to nothing but the finer things. Her version of lying low wasn't hiding out in a safehouse. It was sitting poolside eating caviar. With so many connections the Tolliver family had, it wasn't hard to find the hotel she checked into. He let his money talk from there.

"Where's Boogie?" he asked.

"He's resting," Roz told him, patting Amber's back as she fell back to sleep.

"Well, get him up. He's gon' want to see this," Bentley instructed her and went to the trunk of his car.

"Bentley, this is the first time we've been able to get him to lie down since he was hurt. He really needs to—"

She stopped talking when Bentley lifted the trunk open. Bound inside of it with duct tape over his mouth was Adam staring at her with bugged-out eyes and blood trickling from his temple. His gaze pleaded with her, but she was disgusted just looking at him.

"Like I said, he's gon' want to see this."

The silence was deafening to Adam as he sat in a pitch-black room. His heart pounded against his rib cage because, even though he couldn't see or hear them, he knew he wasn't alone. He knew he was going to die. The only question was how.

The lights suddenly flipped on. Although they weren't bright, he had to squint and blink his eyes to adjust to them. He was finally able to see where he'd been taken to after being dragged out of the trunk. He was in a wine cellar tied to a chair in a wide aisle between the whites and the reds. Leaned against the far wall was Bentley, but he wasn't the one who had turned on the light. Boogie had done that.

He stood at the winding stairs that led to the cellar, staring menacingly at Adam. Even in his injured state, something about him seemed powerful. Not many would have survived what had happened to him. Roz stood beside her man, glaring at Adam. Their hate for him filled the room. Boogie walked slowly over to him and ripped the tape from his mouth.

"Aughh!" he shouted.

"If that's all it takes to make you scream, then we're gon' have a lot of fun," Boogie said, his words coming out breathy.

"Fuck you!"

"I should be the one sayin' that. You're the one who shot *me,* after all."

"I wanted to teach you a lesson."

"There's no lesson in the world I could learn from you except how to not kill a man, because as you can see, I'm still here, little nigga."

"I weakened you, though. The mighty Boogie Tolliver learned that he's not invincible after all. All it took was a 'little nigga' like me to break you."

His words ignited something in Boogie. He swore he saw the fire flash in his eyes right before Boogie's hands were wrapped around his throat. He thought again that he was about to die, but just as he felt himself about to pass out, Boogie let him go. Adam choked for air, and Boogie stumbled back. Roz came to his aid to help stablize him.

"The thing is, I know I'm not invincible. I've seen death so much I know it's inevitable. But a motherfucka like you could never take me out," Boogie said, catching his own breath.

Although he wasn't at full power, he was strong. Adam's aching neck was proof of that. But he didn't care. Staring at him and Roz together he felt the same thing he did the first time he laid eyes on Boogie. He spat at their feet.

"I'll give it to you, you have balls," Boogie chuckled. "I tried to give you an out. Why didn't you take it? And then you tried to kill my daughter, nigga? You gotta pay."

"It looks like you might need a nap first before you do anything," Adam said, continuing to taunt his weakened state, seeing that it had gotten to him before.

"Actually, that's exactly what he's gonna do," Roz spoke up. There was a grim smile on her lips as she stared at Adam. "Oh . . . you thought he was gonna be the one to handle you? Nah. That'll be me."

"And you think that scares me?"

"It should."

"You're the same bitch I broke years ago. Weak."

"I am?" Roz licked her lips and laughed, but it wasn't the kind when something was funny. "You shot my man, you kidnapped my daughter, and now you're weaponizing the trauma you put me through against me. Oh . . . and you tried to smother my baby. My baby? You keep trying to take everything from me. I *hate* you. So I'm gonna make sure you never can hurt me or her again."

"You don't have it in you to kill me."

"I guess we'll find out, huh?" She sneered and spoke to the man on the wall without taking her eyes off Adam. "Bentley, how long did this mother-fucka have my baby?"

"Two days."

"Two days, huh?" Roz stepped forward and leaned down until her lips were by Adam's ear. "There's nothing like a mother scorned. You're going to suffer for two weeks, and before the end of it, you're gonna be *begging* me to kill you."

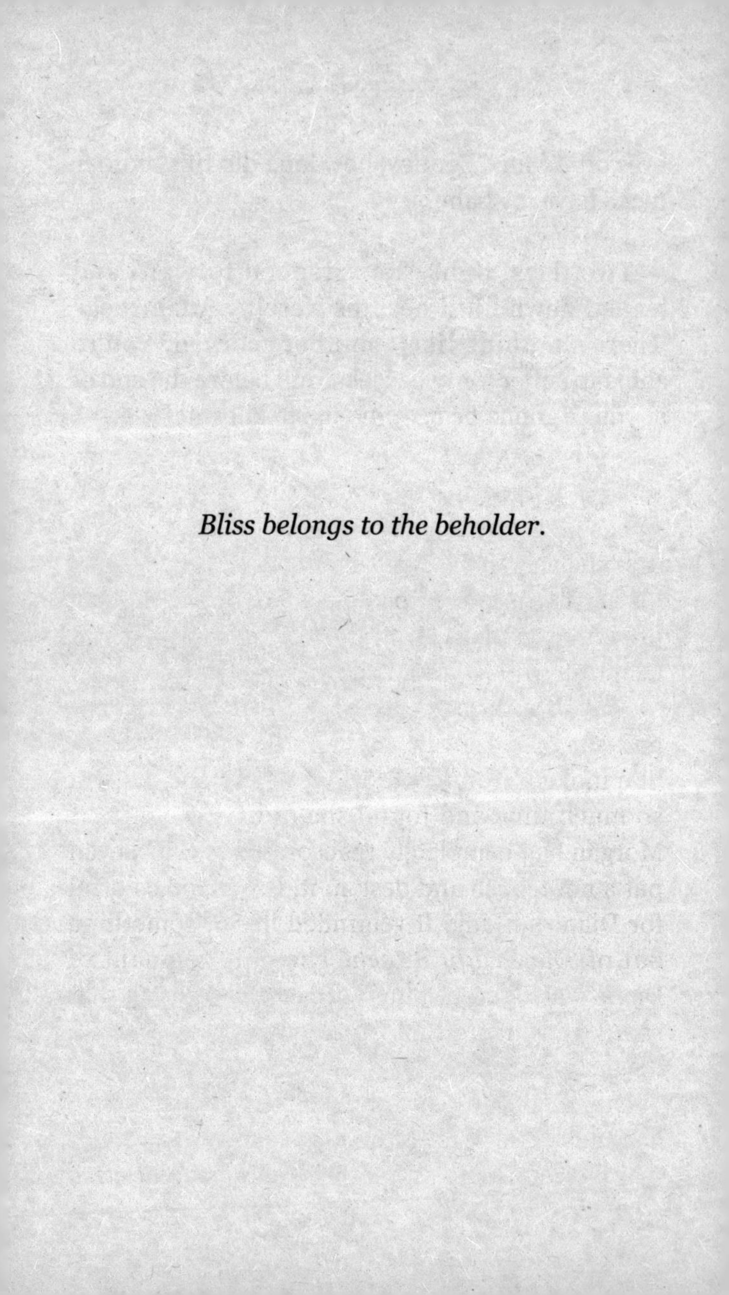

Bliss belongs to the beholder.

Chapter 18

A few days had passed since Diana returned to New York with Caesar. It felt like the last few weeks of her life hadn't even happened. One minute, she was living her best life. The next, reality hit her like a sack of potatoes. Maybe the thought of retirement was an illusion. Either way, it was beautiful while it lasted.

She'd found her way back to the Sugar Trap and sat in the office she'd given up to Morgan. She looked around the room where she'd spent so much time and found she didn't recognize it. Morgan had completely redecorated it. She'd even put a new couch and desk in it. It was too colorful for Diana's liking. It reminded her of something out of *The Brady Bunch*. The only remnant of Diana was a recent photo of her and Morgan that she'd had printed and framed before stepping down.

Diana couldn't say she was sad, because she had moved aside for Morgan to take her place, but that just left Diana wondering where her place was now. She'd come back for Boogie. Seeing him alive and well had done something good for her heart. He would recover fully. However, what about the next time something happened to one of them? She wouldn't be able to drop everything and come running every time. The whole point of her leaving Morgan in charge was so that she could finally move to her own beat. Except she didn't know what her own beat sounded like. Not outside the business of the five families.

Diana sighed as she picked up the handset of the orange rotary phone on the desk and dialed a number. She'd been trying to get in contact with Christina since she'd been back. After learning the gruesome events of what happened in her backyard, Diana wanted to check on her friend. Daniella had been Christina's only daughter, and Diana couldn't imagine losing a child in such a way, especially at the hands of someone like Louisa. There was a time when family killing family was rare, but lately it had been one of the most common things. But what Louisa had done was in cold blood. Diana pressed the phone to her ear and hoped Christina would answer.

"Hello?"

"Christina?" Diana sat up in her seat when she heard the voice.

"No, this is Rosaline," the Alverezes' housekeeper said.

"Oh. Is Christina around? Can you tell her it's Diana?"

There was a slight pause. Diana could swear she heard someone whispering on the other end of the phone. When Rosaline finally came back to the line, she cleared her throat.

"Mrs. Alverez has stepped out for the afternoon. I can take a note."

Diana opened her mouth to tell Rosaline that she knew the woman was lying, but then she thought better of it. What good would it have done? If Christina didn't want to be bothered after experiencing two great losses, then she shouldn't be bothered. Diana would respect it.

"Tell her . . . tell her she's not alone," Diana said and hung up the phone.

Knock! Knock! Seconds after the knock on her door, it opened. She thought it would be Morgan coming to check on her, but it wasn't. Caesar was the one to poke his head inside of the office.

"I thought I would find you here. Mind if I come in?" he asked.

"No, go ahead." She signaled to the seat across from the desk she was seated at.

Caesar walked in and sat down in the pink chair across from her. He got comfortable and adjusted the suit to his tie. Looking around, he wore a small smile on his face. "I really like what you've done with the place," he said.

"Now you know just like I do that I didn't have a damn thing to do with this office! Morgan has the place looking like an Austin Powers movie," Diana groaned. "But she's so proud of it, so I just leave it alone."

"Ahh, parenthood. You gotta love it," Caesar chuckled.

Diana waited patiently for him to get to the point. She knew he wasn't there to check out the new office digs. The moment he sat down, she expected him to go running off at the mouth, but he didn't. Instead, he watched her watching him.

"If I knew I was so interesting, I would sit in front of a mirror all day," Diana said, finally breaking the ice. "Did you need anything, Caesar?"

"No, just came to check on you."

"On me?"

"Of course. You are one of my oldest friends. And I know these last few days haven't been easy on any of us."

"You're right about that. But I'm fine. Boogie's the one you need to be worried about."

"He's doing fine. Better now that they have Amber back."

"Oh, my God! They found her?"

"They got her home," he confirmed, and Diana let out a sigh of relief.

"Oh, that makes me so happy. I'll have to let Morgan know. How?"

"Bentley caught up to the biological father, Adam, and got her back."

"I can't believe that boy didn't call me and tell me."

"I'm sure he would have gotten around to it. He has his hands a little full right now with resting and . . ."

"And what?" Diana asked, noticing how he'd let his voice trail off.

"Notice I didn't say that Bentley killed Adam, because he didn't. He brought him to Boogie so he could have his fun with him."

"Oh." Diana suddenly understood and then groaned. "He should have just killed the son of a bitch and been done with it. Boogie needs to rest."

"Torturing Adam will help him get his strength back up."

"And that's exactly why you aren't a doctor." She shook her head.

"I wouldn't have wanted to be that. I'm too good at what I do. Speaking of that, there's something else I came here to discuss with you."

"Does it have anything to do with Louisa?"

"Yes, how did you know?"

"Just a wild guess."

Diana would have loved nothing more than to sink her claws into Louisa, but she had disappeared in the wind. Diana knew she would turn up one way or another. Something told her that she was still in the city, waiting to attack again.

"Zo called me the other day. He said she wants to meet with him."

"If he goes, I'm going to go with him!"

"No, trust me, we have it all handled," Caesar said, and Diana raised her eyebrow.

"And what does that mean exactly?"

"That you just need to focus on whatever you need to focus on."

"Easier said than done, Caesar. How did he sound. Zo, I mean?"

"Let's just say he's had one hell of a summer so far. He and Boogie both. What happened to Daniella is such a shame. A true tragedy that shouldn't have happened."

"Just watch him, Caesar. You know what happened with Boogie when he first went through what Zo is feeling now."

"Trust me, I remember. And that's why this meeting with Louisa is so important. The best way to kill a cancer is to pull it out by the root so it doesn't spread."

"I'm sorry, sir. It won't happen again," Henry said, and Namir contemplated making a quick example out of him.

"Namir!" a voice boomed, and Namir turned his attention to the owner of it.

He was expecting to see Bosco, but it wasn't him. Instead, it was Matteo, Bosco's younger brother and a man Namir hadn't laid eyes on in years. Matteo hated living in his brother's shadow, so he moved out of state and started a new life, one he could call his own, which was why Namir was even more confused to see him.

"Matteo, what are you doing here? And where the hell is Bosco?"

Matteo glanced quickly at his men and cleared his throat. There was something going on, but Namir couldn't put his finger on it. He couldn't help thinking about the worst-case scenario, and that was Bosco running off with his money. What if Bosco woke up one day and decided to undermine the Lucas name by going against them? It was a less likely possibility, but still it was a possibility.

"How about you come into my office and we discuss everything?" Matteo suggested and led Namir inside the first office space.

Their men stayed put, and Matteo closed the door on them. Namir sat down in a comfortable chair, and Matteo took a seat on top of the desk.

There was an uncomfortable look on his face, but that didn't stop him from starting the conversation.

"If I had been expecting you, then I would have been more prepared, and for that I apologize, Namir."

"It seems you might have a lot to apologize for. Money hasn't been flowing properly. Nothing has been moved in or out of Staten Island for months. So you should have been expecting me." Namir raised a brow at him. "And actually, not you. Your brother. He's been handling my affairs here for the last year while I've been gone. I want to speak to him."

"I'm afraid that won't be able to happen."

"And why not? Where's Bosco?"

"Dead," Matteo told him, and Namir paused for a moment to register that.

"And Eduardo?"

"Dead."

"Stefano too?"

"No, he's alive. He's the one who talked me into coming back. Since we're under new management."

Namir was too stuck on the fact that Bosco was dead and he hadn't heard anything about it until that very second. It was true that Namir had been country hopping, but still, normally news like that traveled fast. He ran a frustrated hand down his face.

"How did Bosco die?"

"He was murdered."

"Fucking murdered? And nobody sent word to me about this?"

"There was no time. Things happened so fast."

"Who would do something so stupid? Don't these motherfuckas know that we're protected?"

"Not anymore. A lot has changed since you decided to go off and explore the world," Matteo sighed. "A war broke out within the families. The pact that so-called kept everything running smoothly on all sides is over. Bosco was just one of the casualties. Caesar killed him."

"Caesar King?"

"The one and only."

"Okay." Namir put praying hands to his lips and processed the information. "I can catch up on all that later. Bosco's dead, fine. What does that have to do with my money?"

"I think it would be best to catch up on everything now. Because . . . then you'll understand why there is no money."

"What the hell do you mean there is no money?" Namir sat up straight in his seat. "How is that even possible?"

"One name. Boogie Tolliver. When all the fighting was going on, the Chinese pulled away from the table when he killed Li."

"Wait," Namir interrupted. "Tolliver as in Barry Tolliver's son?"

"Yes. Barry who's dead, by the way."

"All these motherfuckas dying while I'm gone. Great."

"Barry's death was what ignited the war."

Namir's head was starting to hurt. He'd been gone a single year, and so much had drastically changed. If Matteo weren't telling the story with a straight face, he wouldn't have believed him.

"Okay, continue telling me about this Boogie character."

"When he went to war with the other families, he needed a bigger army. So with Bosco dead—"

"He came to Staten Island to set up shop."

"More than that. He completely took over everything. And he had the manpower to do it."

"You let him?"

"You don't know Boogie. He didn't give Stefano much choice."

"And what did he do to earn your loyalty that quickly? They killed your brother."

"And now I have other family to think about. Boogie did what nobody dared to do. He went to war with every family at the same time, and I think he would have won. That motherfucka isn't somebody you want to cross. He's a monster in human form. I thought he was gonna kill everybody, but then the fighting just seemed to stop."

"So they aren't feuding anymore?"

"No, but like I said, the Chinese pulled away from the table. And with the fifth seat open, I'm sure it's not hard for you to guess what happened next."

"He converted the Romano family."

"Yes, he did. Which means all our money goes that way."

"And what if I just kill you right now for your disloyalty?"

"You could, but that wouldn't change the fact that you won't be making another dime from us." Matteo shrugged. "My advice to you is that maybe you should be more hands-on in business. And a second piece of advice would be to go to the head honcho himself."

Namir wanted nothing more than to put a bullet in the middle of Matteo's eyes, but he didn't. If what Matteo said was true, it wouldn't solve anything. But there was more to it than that. From the moment Namir stepped inside the office, he'd noticed a carelessness about the Italian man. Even while Matteo was explaining, there was no regret in his voice, no fear of consequence. It was almost like he was untouchable. No . . . protected. He couldn't help but think that Matteo even explaining anything was more out of respect than duty.

Namir glared at him and stood. He didn't say a word when he left the office. The moment he stepped out, his men knew to assume the same formation to lead him back to his vehicle. Once he was safely in the back seat of the Wraith, Namir pulled out his phone and dialed a number.

"Son! Did you get that handled on Staten Island?" Nasir Lucas's voice sounded on the other end.

"Dad," Namir sighed, knowing that what he had to say his father wouldn't want to hear. "I'ma tell you what was just told to me. And it's bad."

There's no order in chaos.

Chapter 20

"Ma'am, let me get your bag!"

The voice belonged to a man on Louisa's payroll, Nolan. She'd just stepped off her private jet in Miami, Florida. The air was hot and humid, and she welcomed the beating sun on her tanned skin. She tossed her monogrammed Louis Vuitton Keepall to Nolan and walked on the runway to an awaiting white Range Rover. Once she was in the passenger seat, she touched up her makeup and waited for her luggage to be loaded into the back. One thing Louisa loved was being a beautiful woman, and she would do anything to keep her youth. As she looked in the mirror of the sun visor, she noticed a line underneath her right eye.

"Oh, no you don't," she said and covered it with concealer.

She made a mental note to get it touched up with some Botox while she was in town. After applying another coat of red lipstick, she flipped the visor back up and let out an impatient sigh. She was growing bored with the scenery around her and wanted to leave.

"You aren't finished yet?"

"Almost, Louisa. We just didn't expect you to come back with so many things," Nolan said as he and another stacked the last of her bags in the back. "We would have readied a different vehicle if we knew."

"Shopping always helps me when I have a lot on my mind."

"I see." Nolan got into the car and looked back at the jet as if he were waiting for someone else to step off. "No Daniella?"

It was the first time since she had died that someone had spoken her name in Louisa's presence. It would have been nice to say that she felt some sort of remorse from killing her only niece, but she didn't. There was no regret. When Louisa heard the heartfelt way that Zo was talking to Daniella, she realized that he probably wouldn't stop at anything to get her back. He wanted Daniella to see his love for her and their family, and eventually Louisa knew Daniella would see it. Not only did that make her a liability, but it also meant she would choose someone else over her, just like Marco had. The only reasonable thing to do at that point was to kill Daniella. If Louisa couldn't have her, no one could. She thought about killing Christina too so Zo would understand what it felt like to be all alone, but what Louisa had up her sleeve was much sweeter.

"She won't be coming, now or ever."

"Oh," Nolan said and then understood what the words meant. "*Oh.*"

"Never speak her name to me again."

"She's already forgotten." Nolan gestured as if he were throwing something out the window before driving off.

"Good. How is my money looking?"

"Up ten percent from last week."

"Good. What about weapons and drugs distro?"

"All orders went out three days ago. There is one little problem."

"And that is?"

"G Baby in Little Haiti. He's claiming we shorted him again. He just got his order today."

"Again? Hmm, that seems to insinuate that there was a first time."

"Never. The little fuck is just trying to get more for nothing. I don't even know why we do business with that hood trash. I say we clear them out completely and take the territory."

"As appealing as that sounds, I've already ignited one war. I don't have the time to entertain another."

"So what do you want to do? They're talking about retaliation."

"Take me to him."

"Now?"

"Right now."

Nolan called back to the SUV following them and told them that they were switching destinations and to follow them. He also told them to make sure they were on high alert due to the territory they were traveling in. G Baby was young, about 25, and rough around the edges. He wasn't one to be fooled with, and on Louisa's rise to power, she made it her job to know who Miami's heavy hitters were. She wanted them on her side or on no side. G Baby was just one of those people nobody could tame no matter how hard a person tried, so instead, she just kept him in check. Everyone knew that Louisa was the biggest weapons and drugs connect in all of Florida. Being on her bad side was like standing in front of a train as it passed. You just didn't want to do it, and she was going to remind him.

G Baby and his crew were at one of the main stash houses they did business at. It was a peach-colored one-story house, and Louisa spotted G Baby's green Camaro parked in front of it. Every house surrounding was either abandoned or owned by G Baby's crew. It was almost the perfect setup. Nolan parked the SUV and got out to open Louisa's door. Her Bottega Veneta wire-stretch heels graced the concrete, and she smoothed out her formfitting skirt suit when she stood up.

As she began walking to the front door, the men from the SUV following hers got out and rushed to her. There were eight in total, and they filed behind and to the sides of her. When she got to the porch, she saw someone peek out quickly from the blinds of the window, and Louisa waved at the camera on the porch ceiling. Suddenly, two black men appeared on the flanks of the house. They were identical twins. Both had long braids and chocolate skin. The intimidating tattoos on their faces were probably the only indicator of who was who. They pointed automatic weapons toward Louisa and her entourage, giving them an evil stare. Louisa's men drew their own weapons and prepared for a gunfight if need be. Louisa told her men to hold it by putting her hand up.

"Maybe you two were on a lunch break, but the whole purpose of having you outside is to make sure people don't make it up here." Louisa pointed at where she stood on the porch. "But since I've made it this far, be dolls and have G Baby open the fucking door."

The twins didn't say a word. In fact, they didn't even look at each other. One of them pulled a walkie-talkie from his pocket and radioed inside. Louisa couldn't hear what he said into it, but moments later, the front door opened, and there stood a shirtless G Baby holding an AR pistol. He was a young man, but the wrinkles on his face aged him about ten years. He wore his locs in thick wicks and had a mouth full of gold teeth. From the pissed-off expression he wore without trying to hide it, Louisa could tell that he wasn't thrilled about having her on his doorstep.

"G Baby, just the man I wanted to see," Louisa said, smiling.

She ignored his guns and gently pushed him out of the way with her fingers so she could step inside. Nolan and four of her men stepped in with her and cased the place like a Section 8 inspection. G Baby hadn't been in the house alone. There were two others seated at a table against the wall, placing money in a money counter. In the center of the table was a pile of kilos of cocaine.

"Louisa, you can't be just showin' up at my shit like this," G Baby said in a deep baritone voice.

"I can when you're accusing me of shorting you." Louisa smiled pleasantly, and G Baby glanced quickly at the table with the drugs.

"Yeah." G Baby balled his fists. "I paid for fifteen kilos, and your mans here dropped off ten."

"And why didn't you address it in the moment?" Louisa asked.

"'Cause. We been doin' business for so long, I thought I could trust you."

"You should know to never trust anyone in this line of business. Well, I'm here now. Let's get it corrected. Let me count the kilos in the order you just got today. I'm sure you haven't cut it yet."

Louisa stood patiently and watched an uncomfortable expression come over G Baby's face. She knew by the wrapping of the kilos on the table that they were hers, so she made a step toward them. G Baby sidestepped in front of her, and to her surprise, there was a sneer there.

"You don't have to count anything. I told you it was short, and that's all you need to know."

She wished that she could say she was surprised by his bravado, but she wasn't. In fact, she expected it, especially since her eyes had already counted the fifteen kilos on the table. One thing about Louisa was that she didn't like to lose money or just give it away. Behind G Baby, she saw the men snatch shotguns from the bottom of the table.

"You made a mistake by comin' here, *chica*. You might think you run Miami, but right now this is *my* kingdom. And you just walked into a bear's den."

"Funny. That's my favorite animal." Louisa smirked right before she made her move.

She snatched G Baby's weapon from his hands and put the muzzle under his chin. It wasn't hard to do. One thing she noticed about a lot of men was that they couldn't multitask. While G Baby was busy trying to intimidate her, she saw the grip on his gun loosen, making him vulnerable, and Louisa loved a vulnerable man. They were the easiest to conquer. Louisa's men had their pistols pointed at the other two men who had jumped to their feet. When they saw what the odds were, they reluctantly lowered their shotguns.

"Bitch!" G Baby grumbled.

"I get that a lot." Louisa flashed her pearly whites. "You just ruined a good thing for yourself, G Baby. Your operation isn't even big enough for me to give you so many kilos, but I do because I know you can sell it. But you see where my niceness got me? I am trying to feed you a feast, but you are gluttonous. You should have repaid my generosity with loyalty, but instead you pay me in deceit. And now here we are."

"We should have taken you out a long time ago."

"Except you can't, can you?" Louisa taunted him and kissed his cheek, leaving red lipstick on his dark skin. "Nobody is dumb enough to do what you have done. Take the men behind you for example. They stood down instantly. If it were I in your shoes, my men would have lit this entire house up with no regard for themselves. They would die for me. And if your men won't die for you, what makes you think they'd go to war for you?"

He was quiet. Yet another way Louisa liked for men to be. There was no doubt about it—she had grown addicted to the power she held. G Baby's heart was still inside his body, but she felt like she was holding it in the palm of her hand. It was a beautiful and yet terrifying thing, having control over whether someone lived or died. And of course the answer with him was simple. He had to die. She squeezed the trigger of the AR pistol one time.

The shot was loud, and she watched the bullet enter through G Baby's chin and exit out the top of his head. His blood painted the ceiling, and a couple splatters got on her cheek.

Louisa watched as he collapsed to the ground, dead, and on her cue, her men fired on the two men by the table, killing them instantly. Louisa dropped the gun by G Baby's body and turned around to exit the house.

"The drugs," Nolan reminded her.

"Leave them," she said and left the house. Outside, the twins had been disarmed and were standing to the side, visibly shaken. It didn't take a neuroscientist to realize what had just happened. Louisa stared at them and pointed. "You two. This is your operation now. Show me that two heads are better than one."

"Yes, ma'am," they replied in unison.

"Clean that mess up and do damage control on the block. If they saw something, be very convincing when you tell them they didn't."

With that, she and her men got back into their vehicles. As Nolan pulled away, Louisa noticed a few blood droplets on her pink skirt. She groaned out loud and envisioned killing G Baby a second time. As irritation crept up on her slowly, she reminded herself that she was finally on the way home. The thought of what was waiting for her cleared away all feelings of disdain.

***

A beautiful melodic voice sang through the speakers in her room as Louisa sashayed back inside her room from the connecting balcony. That night, there was a cool breeze that whipped her sheer robe up, revealing that she had on nothing but lingerie. In her hand was a glass of champagne, her third of the night, and it wouldn't be her last. As she walked back to her canopy bed, she moved her hips to the music, enjoying her buzz.

"Did you enjoy the view, my love?" The voice belonged to a handsome brown man lying in her bed with his head propped up on his hand.

His name was Alejandro Valdez, an immigrant from Mexico whom Louisa had made the foolish mistake of falling in love with. She had no idea how she'd allowed it to happen. One minute she was hiring a driver to get her to and fro, and the next she was in bed with him. Alejandro was twenty years younger than her, but he could keep up with her, and she with him. He made Louisa feel things in places she didn't know existed. With every other man in her past, it had just been about sex. An orgasm was the only emotion she was willing to allow a man to have of hers. However, Alejandro came through like a construction man and tore down all the walls she'd put in place to protect herself.

It was hard to let him in at first, especially since the only man she'd ever loved was her brother,

Marco. She'd never been *in* love with anybody because everyone close to her had hurt her deeply. Even Marco had when he chose Christina and his kids over her. But Alejandro was different. He was hers. She was in the process of getting him his green card so he would never be taken away from her. Louisa was scared to lose him, which was why she kept him a secret from everyone, even Nolan. Marco also hadn't been told about him when he was alive. He'd become the closest thing to her heart, and that meant he was her weakness.

"It was beautiful. Did you know the moon was full tonight?" She giggled and got in bed with him.

"I haven't paid attention to anything except you all evening," he said, kissing her lips.

Alejandro took the wineglass away from her and placed it on the nightstand on his side of the bed. The two of them spent the next couple of minutes lying down and staring into each other's eyes. There was a softness and vulnerability that Louisa didn't know was inside of her. He was so beautiful with his dark brown hair and chiseled face. His lips had a natural pout that made her want to kiss them all the time. He must have been reading her mind, because the next thing she knew, his lips were on hers again. He kissed her deeply. Their tongues intertwined in a dance of passion until she came up for air.

"I missed you," he said to her with his thick accent, and she smiled.

"I missed you too. I wish I could be here with you all the time."

"Then why don't you? You don't need to be out there all the time. What you do is dangerous."

"Alejandro, we've been over this many times. My business is what affords us this lifestyle."

"I don't need a luxury lifestyle to be happy. I just need you."

"Really?" she asked dreamily.

"I would not lie to you, my love. But . . ." Alejandro sat up in the bed and sighed.

"But what?" Louisa jolted up, noticing the frustrated look on his face.

"I don't know if I can do this, Louisa. You always have me in the house. I never get out. I can't live like this."

"I keep you in the house to keep you safe. I don't want anything to happen to you because of me."

"And what do you expect of me? To live like this forever because you are so busy chasing money?"

"We can't live without money, Alejandro."

"And when will you have enough money, Louisa? I don't think you are running the show anymore. I think you are addicted to it. And if you continue to choose that life over the one you can have with me, then . . ."

"Then what?" Louisa asked when his voice trailed off. "What are you trying to say, Alejandro, that you don't want to be with me?"

"That's not what I'm saying at all. I love you, Louisa. What I'm saying is your decisions are selfish, and they are making choices for me."

Louisa could tell that he was serious. She also could not deny the fact that he was right. It was inevitable that the day a man like him would grow tired of being in the house. No matter how vast and beautiful Louisa's home was, the world would always be more appealing. She finally had found someone who chose her, and she was pushing him away. She took a deep breath and took his hand in hers.

"I promise you, Alejandro, I choose you. I swear to you. I have some business to wrap up in New York—"

Alejandro sighed loudly.

"I'm in the middle of business there," she continued, "but once I'm done, I will be all yours. I'll leave it all behind. But I have to go back. I flew here just to see you, though, because I missed you so much. Does that not count for anything?"

The part about her reason for flying back to Miami was the truth. She'd taken Marco's private jet to go home because she missed Alejandro terribly. Plus, it was hot in the city for her, but he didn't need to know the details about that. The part that she lied about was getting out of the game. He was right about one thing—she was addicted to money. It was something she wouldn't give up, but they could cross that path when they got there. After she did what she planned to do in Queens, she would give Alejandro the best months of his life. It would be a temporary fix, but a fix nonetheless.

"Okay, *mi amore*. I'll hold you to that promise." Alejandro flashed her his perfect smile and pulled her to him. "Right now, I want you to show me exactly how much you missed me."

Time heals all wounds.

—Menander

Chapter 21

As the days passed, Boogie's strength came back to him. Everybody around him was telling him to rest, but staying still wasn't something he was good at. The only thing he wanted to do was get back in the action, not watch it on television. So he stopped taking his pain medication and relied on natural herbs and water to heal his body. He began eating more, even when he didn't feel like he had an appetite. When he felt strong enough, he started going on walks around the property and building up his endurance. When he felt that he could lift, he hit the weights. It wasn't what any physical therapist would have suggested, but he didn't care. It was painful at first, especially without his medication, but he ate the pain like the beast he was. Soon he grew accustomed to the feeling and was able to work through it without wincing. He still had a little ways to go on the road to recovery, but when he was able to get back in the streets, he wouldn't be a shadow of who he used to be. He would still be Bryshon Tolliver.

Just like other mornings since he'd gotten back active, Boogie found himself in the gym of the Big House finishing his workouts. His determination drowned out his body telling him it was tired. He would rest after breakfast, but he refused to miss out on any time he could be using to strengthen his body. And he realized the best time was when Roz and Amber were sleeping. He really didn't want to hear Roz's mouth, so he always tried to be done before she woke up. He chugged the remaining water in his bottle and prepared to head up to shower.

"You sure it's safe for you to be working that hard?"

He didn't have to turn around to know Caesar had entered the gym, but he did anyway. "If you tell Roz, I'll have to hunt you down and kill you, old man," Boogie said, looking like a deer caught in headlights.

"Your secret is safe with me," Caesar said and chuckled. "But seriously, you should be taking it easy."

"I can't. The world didn't stop when I got shot, so I gotta catch up to it."

"Understood. Have you at least talked to Jillian?"

"You mean the nurse you gave my number to? Yes. She's been callin' me every day like a stalker."

"Well, what does she say about all this?" Caesar motioned his hands around the gym.

"She told me it's safe to work out, just to know my limits."

"Don't go too hard. I know you're ready to jump back into the action, but this is the part where you have to trust the people around you. Do you?"

"Trust my people? Hell yeah. They stood by me during all this bullshit. It's just hard. I mean, you understand. You were in my position not too long ago."

"I do understand. But I also let my body heal while somebody else ran the show for a while." Caesar raised a brow in a knowing way, and Boogie sighed.

"You think I'm rushin' it?"

"I think God has given you time. Quality time that you can very well be spending with your loved ones. Because when you jump back in the game, who knows when you'll have this kind of time again?"

Boogie had been so focused on getting back to 100 percent that he hadn't even taken a moment to think about what Caesar had just said. He was right. They'd just gotten Amber back, and Boogie should have been spending every waking minute bonding with her. He was so busy thinking about getting out there and making sure that what happened to her would never happen again that he hadn't celebrated her safe return.

On top of that, Adam was still locked away in the wine cellar. Boogie should have been checking on Roz's mental state whenever he could. Days had gone by, and she hadn't gone back to the cellar. She wouldn't let anybody else go either. He thought it was part of her punishment for him, so he did as she wished. Still, he needed to sit her down and see where her head was at. He was sure she'd never killed anyone before. It changed a person.

"Why do you always gotta show up makin' so much sense, man?" Boogie groaned.

"Because if I don't, who will? Come on, I'll make you some breakfast."

Boogie's stomach growled loudly on cue. He was happy that his appetite was back for the most part because he hated forcing himself to eat. Caesar patted him on his sweaty back, and the two of them left the gym, headed for the kitchen. He didn't know if he had ever said it out loud, but Boogie was glad he had someone like Caesar to guide him, especially during so many ups and downs in his life. Learning about Caesar's past made Boogie look at him in a different light. By age 18, Caesar was an orphan. He had to grow and guide himself. Boogie found himself thinking about the story Caesar had told him. He glanced over at him as they walked and gave him a curious look.

"Yo, Caesar. Whatever happened to that Nasir cat from back in your day? I've never heard you talk about him until recently. He still around?"

"Nasir?" At first Caesar seemed thwarted by the question. His eyes grew dark but then went normal again. "That's right, I never told you the rest of the story."

"Yeah. You left off with your dad's murder, and after that, the pact was formed."

"That's right. The pact was formed shortly after that, but there were a few happenings in between. I guess now is as good a time as any to tell you what happened to the Grim Reaper."

It's not in you, it's on you.

Chapter 22

The Past

"Baby, aren't you gonna eat?"

Caesar knew that Amira was talking to him, but he was too consumed by his own thoughts to respond. Martina had fixed them smothered chicken for dinner, one of his favorites, but he found himself pushing his food around his plate with a fork. Admittedly, Martina was trying everything to get Caesar to eat, but he just didn't have an appetite. He was still wrapping his head around the fact that he would never experience his father's presence again. Outside of the home, he showed no signs of weakness due to that fact, but behind the walls of his family home it wasn't so easy to pretend. The deaths of Joseph and Ed hadn't even eased his pain. Not in the slightest bit.

"Caesar?" That time when Amira spoke, Caesar looked up from his plate.

"Yeah?"

"Are you okay?" she asked, and then a sheepish look came over her face. "I'm sorry. Of course you aren't okay. Grieve as long as you want, baby. Just please eat something."

Caesar's plan had been to buy Amira her own house, but things changed after Cassius died. She moved into the mansion shortly after the funeral, and whereas Caesar was thankful for the company, sometimes he just needed silence.

"I'm not hungry," he finally answered her.

"That's the sadness talking. But your body needs food to keep up your strength. Plus, Martina keeps cooking all this food for you to cheer you up."

"Nothing can cheer me up," Caesar said, not meaning to sound as dry as he did, but he also didn't care to clear it up.

"Maybe if you just try—"

"Dammit, I'm not hungry! How many times do I have to say it to be heard?" Caesar's fist pounded on the table, and Amira jumped. "I wish everyone would just leave me alone."

"Okay," she said softly.

When Caesar looked up at her, he saw that she was genuinely hurt. It wasn't just her expression that said it, but the tears in her eyes spoke to him. He instantly felt lower than dirt. She was just trying to be there for him. He opened his mouth to apologize, but she put her hand up to stop him and ran from the table.

"Dammit!" he said again and put his face in his hands.

He groaned loudly. Nothing around him was going right. His grief was beginning to consume him the exact same way it did when his mother was buried. Nothing and nobody in life could prepare a person for losing a parent. It was just a big bag of pain you carried wherever you went, never putting it down, no matter how heavy it got. It was a losing battle, especially with the entire King empire falling on his shoulders. He needed the cards in his hand to be reshuffled because he didn't know what to do with them.

The sound of someone clearing his throat took Caesar's attention from his own thoughts. Standing in the wide doorway of the kitchen was Donald, the King family butler. He was an elderly black man, older than Cassius had been, who always wore a black suit. His hands were clasped and resting on top of his belly as he waited patiently to be acknowledged.

"What is it, Donald? Don't you see that I'm eating?" Caesar asked, and Donald raised a curious brow as he glanced at his untouched plate.

"I am sorry to interrupt your, uh, dinner, sir. But there is someone here to see you."

Caesar groaned. He had half a mind to tell Donald to send away whoever it was. In his mind, he could only guess that the person was another family member coming to check on him. Niles's mother had been the worst of the bunch. Every time he looked up, she was at his door. He sighed. "Who is it?"

"He gave me the name Nasir Lucas. Should I tell him you are busy?"

"No, it's okay. Take him to the main sitting area. I'll be there in a second."

"Of course, sir."

Donald left, and Caesar stood up from the table. He was dressed formally, as he always was. His father taught him when he was young that a businessman always dressed ready for business. Except at that moment Caesar didn't know what kind of business Nasir was there on. He hadn't heard from him since the funeral. But then again, if he and Cassius were business partners, then Nasir getting in contact should have been expected.

Caesar left the kitchen and went to what his mother used to call the "white room." The name itself was telling. Everything in it was white except for the crystal decor all around it. She decorated it herself and made it off-limits. But when she died, it was hard for him and his father to stay out of it. It was like the white room was the only place in the whole house to carry on her essence, an essence that Caesar needed right that second. When he got there, Nasir was seated patiently on one of the comfortable couches with his arms spread across the top and his legs crossed.

"Caesar!" Nasir stood up upon his arrival.

"Nasir." Caesar shook his hand before the two men sat down across from each other. "Can I get you anything? Refreshments, maybe something to drink?"

"No, thank you. But I have to say, you are more hospitable than your father ever was," Nasir tried to joke but Caesar didn't smile. "I apologize. It's too soon."

"Don't worry about it. It's going to take me a while to get used to him being gone."

Nasir studied Caesar with what almost seemed to be a concerned look on his face. "How are you holding up, Caesar?"

"Whatever is expected of a man in my position is what I am," Caesar answered flatly.

"I'm not asking how Caesar the boss is doing, I'm asking about Caesar the person."

"I never placed you to be the sentimental type."

"When it comes to the sake of my business, I can be. Because as you know, your father and I were partners. Which means that now you and I are partners. And knowing how you are is important to me."

It was Caesar's turn to study him. He was trying to find his angle. But Nasir seemed genuinely interested in seeing where his head was at.

"I guess . . ." Caesar racked his mind trying to find the right words. "Do you know what's crazy?

Pretty much my entire life I knew I would take over the family business one day. I knew that I would be in charge of everything, but I thought I would have more time."

"With Cassius?"

"Yes. It took his dying for me to realize that I never truly thought the day would come." Caesar laughed in spite of himself. "A mortal man I knew would die one day, but I was still shocked when it happened."

"Does that make you feel great sorrow?"

"Only a man without a soul wouldn't grieve the death of his father," Caesar said, looking into Nasir's eyes. "But to succumb to that sadness would be disrespectful to his legacy. He was the king. I was the prince. Now I'm the king and nothing else will fall. I'm sure you heard what happened to the men responsible."

"I did. I was impressed by how quickly you found out who was behind the deed."

"I'm a thorough man. I'm not one to let these kind of things fester."

"It's a shame they won't ever get brought to justice. I know the cops were thirsty for some kind of bust."

"I got my own justice."

"What I can't quite understand is how exactly you found out who was behind it."

"Let's just say they should have used a revolver."

"Fascinating. You know, the day your father brought you to meet me, I wondered why he had waited so long to introduce us. At first, I thought it was because he didn't think you were ready, which could very well be true. But now I understand that he was keeping his best kept secret. He truly bred and brought up the ultimate boss. And you're so young still."

Nasir had an intrigued look across his face. It was like he was seeing Caesar for the first time. Caesar couldn't tell what the thoughts were behind his eyes, but he could see something happening.

"I always find it funny when people are intrigued by my age," Caesar said. "Maybe it's because I don't feel young. I never really got to enjoy my youth the way other boys did. My body is eighteen, but my mind is double that. But still, men only see my body, and they don't care about my mind. And that's why everything I do is unexpected by them. That enlists their fear. It makes them see and respect me."

"Now *I* didn't place you to be like your father in that way."

"Because I'm not. My father purposefully did things to make everyone around him fear him. I simply am myself."

"Powerful." Nasir tapped his chin as he took in Caesar's words. "You impress me every time you speak. I look forward to doing business with you, and I hope you look to me as I did to your father. As a kind of mentor of sorts."

"I guess that just depends on you."

"That it does. I'll be in touch. But before I leave, I have a question for you. Before Cassius was killed, he was attempting what I consider a hostile takeover of the other territories. He had a plan, a crazy one. But it might have worked had he lived. Do you plan on continuing where he left off?"

"No," Caesar said.

It was a short answer, but the truth. Nasir eyed him curiously, like he knew he was hiding something, but Caesar kept his poker face. He *did* have something up his sleeve, but it wasn't to take over anyone's territory. Cassius's plan was callous and almost evil. Caesar didn't see any kind of peaceful resolve in it. All he could see were the other families joining forces to eventually overthrow him. And that thought was what honestly sparked an idea. It might have been crazier than Cassius's, but in Caesar's mind it was better. In fact, with the help of Damián, Caesar had successfully set up a meeting with the heads of the other families, something he had decided against telling anyone about. Not even Amira knew, and at that second, he thought better of telling Nasir.

"Good," Nasir said and stood. "I should be going now. I look forward to doing business with you."

Caesar walked Nasir to the front door. He watched as he got in his car and drove away. Something about the conversation with him made Caesar remember that, although he had suffered a great loss, he still had much to look forward to. He just had to switch his mindset from thinking that the glass was half empty when it was actually half full.

He thought about Amira upstairs probably pouting, and he smiled, not at her pain, but at how hard she was going to make getting back into her good graces. She would forgive him though, especially when he came upstairs with a bowl of her favorite ice cream.

Sometimes it's the winner who has to wave the white flag.

Chapter 23

The Past

It didn't dawn on Caesar how risky what he was attempting was. Not until he, Niles, and a handful of Caesar's men were filing out of their vehicles. Damián Alverez, Domino Reyes, Wang Lei Chen, and Benjamin Tolliver had all agreed to meet Caesar that afternoon. The designated meeting place was The Museum of Fine Black Arts. It was one of Caesar's favorite places to go with his mother when he was a boy. But that wasn't why he chose it. He chose it because the museum was located in Central Park, which was always busy. Caesar figured he would run less chance of something bad happening that way. Still, they were all still so unpredictable.

"I don't know how I always let you talk me into doin' this crazy shit," Niles said, making sure his gun was concealed under his pea coat.

"You're here because somewhere in that heart of yours you love little ol' me," Caesar replied with a grin.

"So what does that say about you, huh? You can't love me if you're always puttin' me in situations where I could *die!*"

Caesar laughed. He knew Niles was just talking mess, because one thing about his cousin was that he would follow him into the depths of hell if he had to. That was just how loyal he was. He and Caesar walked side by side toward the museum's back entrance. The others with them followed closely behind. The museum had a strict no-gun policy, but Caesar would be damned if he went inside without it. They were spotted as soon as they entered the museum and were waved over to the far right by an older gentleman. In his hand was a metal detector, which he began waving up and down over all their bodies. Caesar knew that although they all were packing, the detector wouldn't make a sound.

"How's the family, Paul?" he asked when the last of his men was checked.

"Everyone is good. Michelle, though, she's been worried about you since your old man died. How you been, son?"

See, Caesar had known Paul since he was just a boy. He had been good friends with Caesar's parents and was someone who could be trusted. He had taken a liking to Caesar and had shown him all the secrets in the museum, including a crawl space that led to the back of the building, which Caesar used a few times to scare his mother silly.

The concern in Paul's eyes was sincere, and Caesar wondered if Paul saw the man he had become or the bright-eyed kid he once had been.

"Just taking things a day at a time."

"I heard that. Well, let me be the one to say you've grown into quite the young man," Paul told him. "When you called and said you needed the conference room today, I cleared out every other reservation. I set it up real nice for you. Just go straight and then . . . I don't even know why I'm giving you directions. You know the way!"

"I do. Thanks again." He walked past him, and his entourage followed.

Caesar led them down a long hall in the back of the old building toward a set of tall double doors. Standing along the walls were four small groups of men staring each other down. Each group was a different ethnicity, and Caesar didn't have to guess why they were there.

"Niles, you come in with me, and the rest of you stay out here and make sure nobody causes any trouble," Caesar instructed his men as he and Niles stepped inside the conference room.

If it weren't for their men in the hall, Caesar would have been shocked to see Damián, Wang Lei,

Domino, and Benjamin already seated at the table. It seemed as though Caesar was late to his own party. The seat at the head of the rectangular table was vacant, so Caesar sat in it. Niles took a seat on the wall away from the table. The room was so quiet a pin could be heard if it dropped. Everyone beside Damián stared at Caesar with impatient eyes, waiting for him to speak.

"What was so important that we had to meet so urgently?" Wang Lei asked with annoyance seeping from his thick accent.

"What the Chinaman said," Benjamin threw in. "I don't like being anywhere when I feel like I'm surrounded by enemies."

"Your only enemy is your sticky-ass fingers," Wang Lei spat at him. "I have not forgotten what you have done."

"I figured you wouldn't. You motherfuckas live to be a hundred years old and never forget a thing. But this best be something you put behind you."

"Never. What your camp took from me is irreplaceable. You are nothing but a bunch of low-life thieves!"

"Well, I guess that makes you a low-life killer. No real knack for anything, so you just kill people for money. Ha! It doesn't get any lower than that."

With the two of them going back and forth, the meeting had already started off on a bad note. Caesar hoped that it wouldn't foil his plan for them all. His eyes fell on a painting on the wall. It was one of his favorites as a kid. It used to be out on display, but the museum staff had moved it inside the conference room. It was of a black man sitting on stage playing a saxophone. He remembered as a kid making his own name for the painting: *The Saxophone Man*. He used to wonder how someone had been able to add all the intricate details with a paintbrush. He blinked away from the painting and focused back on the men bickering before him. He interrupted them by clearing his throat and waited until everyone's eyes were back on him.

"I know you all are wondering why I called you here today. I also know that some of your business dealings with my father were not on the pleasant side. Nevertheless, I want to thank you for meeting me."

"I am only here because Damián is cashing in on a favor I owe him. And I must warn you, you only have five minutes of my time," Wang Lei said.

"That works for me because that's all the time I need to put my proposition on the table. It's something that I think will benefit each person at this table mutually."

"Proposition?" Domino asked.

Domino was a slender man with a muscular build. He was what women called easy on the eyes and wore his long hair pulled back into a braided ponytail. He ran his business out of Harlem, and although that was in the Kings' territory, they never stepped on each other's toes. Domino dabbled in the business of women, and it was a fact that Cassius's people were some of his best clients. It also was a fact that Domino was not to be underestimated. His family stood strong and had the numbers to back it up. The arrangement between the Reyes family and the King family had a little part to play in what Caesar was putting on the table.

"I'm going to be straightforward with all of you," Caesar continued, placing his arms on the table as he leaned forward. "I'm tired of fucking fighting. It's just a show of ego that costs everybody money. We all are guilty of this bullshit, and if we continue like this, it will just show how stupid we are."

"You're just a boy. Who the hell are you to sit at this table and speak to us like that?" Benjamin spoke in a bull-like manner. "We've been running things just fine since you were in diapers."

His voice was deep and his smooth skin as black as a dark chocolate Hershey's bar. The short Afro graying on the top of his head was the only indicator of his age. The dour look on his face told Caesar that he wasn't too happy about being called stupid.

"You call this fine? Let me ask all of you this: how many of your loved ones have you lost at the hands of someone at this table? And if not them, someone in their camp." Just like Caesar figured, nobody said anything. "And the saddest part is I'm sure nobody even remembers who threw the first blow. We've been at each other's throats for so long that the blame has gotten lost somewhere in limbo. I'm calling for a cease-fire."

"This is the perfect time to say you remind me of somebody I know," Benjamin told him. "Oh! That's right. His name was Cassius King. Bloodthirsty for control and always wanting things his way. What the hell is a cease-fire going to do?"

"It's going to give us time to sort some things out. And, Benjamin, I might look like my father, but I promise you we are two completely different men. I've been breathing this business for as long as I can remember. I'm not here in this seat for no reason."

"Ha! What do you really know? You're just a boy like I said."

"He's a boy who happens to be right," Damián stepped in. "Listen to what he has to say, all of you. You might learn a thing or two. Continue, Caesar."

"If I offended any of you with my words, that truly was not my intention. I just need you to see, like I've been able to see, how foolish we've been. My age has nothing to do with that fact. And, Benjamin, I'm here to stay, so you might as well get used to seeing my young face. We sit here as the five most powerful families in New York, yet we are divided. Why do you think that is?"

"Greed," Domino said.

"Power," Wang Lei offered.

"Yes and yes. Everybody wants to do everything. Everyone except Domino here. He knows his place and where things for him are most lucrative. He has never tried to venture out of that and, because of it, has feuded the least."

"This is true," Domino agreed.

"Damián, you know why you and my father got into it all the time, don't you? You are the only one in the state who can bring in military-grade weapons while the rest of us are left with metal scraps. So why have you tried to sell drugs, too, knowing that the Kings have the best connect on the East Coast? You can't compete. It's like a slap in the face when you try." Caesar turned to Benjamin. "And you. Everyone knows that the Tolliver riches come from all the high-end robberies you commit all over the world. What you do is more than thievery. It's an art to be envied. But committing the crimes against us is something that shouldn't be done. You put a target on your entire family's back that way. Isn't that why someone hired one of Wang Lei's hit men to come after you?"

"Yeah," Benjamin sighed.

"Wang Lei, you have some of the most dangerous assassins working for you, and I also know that you are the man people go to when they need any kind of loan. Why not open your services to the other boroughs, not just the Bronx? Why don't we *all* open our territories to each other? Individually we will always be capped, but the money we could make together would be endless!"

"So what are you proposing? Some sort of truce?" Benjamin asked.

"No, what I want to put on the table is something that can't be broken. I'm proposing a pact. Not just any pact. One signed in blood."

"And what will this pact decree?"

"One of the conditions will be that we all agree to one form of business, so that way nobody steps on each other's toes. Another is that we are all protected. No family shall harm another family, and if anyone in your camp disobeys this rule, they will either be exiled or killed by you, the head of the organization. Other specifics can be worked out, because I want all of you to have a say-so in something so big and life-changing. But ultimately this is a change that needs to happen. We've fought for so long. Why don't we try peace for a while?"

When he was done speaking, the room grew quiet again. To the left of Caesar, Damián had a tiny approving smile on his face. However, it was the others Caesar was worried about. If even one of them didn't agree, it never would work. Without them all coming together, the fighting would continue, and Caesar would have wasted his time and breath.

Finally, Benjamin cleared his throat.

"I might have been wrong to prejudge you, Caesar King. You've done what none of us could do, and that's something as simple as getting us all to sit down together. And I'm even more impressed that the words that came out of your mouth weren't complete bullshit. In all my time, nobody has even thought of doing something like that. And as crazy as it sounds, it might work."

"It *will* work if we make it," Caesar said confidently. "If we put all our differences behind us, I mean truly put them behind us, we will be unstoppable. Why should there be one throne when there can be five equally powerful ones? It just makes sense. But I also know I can't force anyone here to see reason."

When Caesar was done speaking, the room grew quiet again. His eyes darted around the room as he hoped they would see reason. However, the silence was deafening.

"I think we should at least try it out," Domino's voice finally sounded to Caesar's relief. "If everyone else does, I will agree to this pact. But as you said, other kinks will need to be worked out."

"I will agree to the pact!" Damián was next to approve.

"I'll agree to this as well, especially if it will get those Chinese motherfuckas off my ass," Benjamin said and stared crossly at Wang Lei. "I'll even give back the necklace and bracelet we stole."

"This is something that I will need to think about," Wang Lei said. "I have never thought of aligning myself with any of you. It isn't a decision that I can make lightly."

"How about I give you two weeks to make your decision?" Caesar asked.

"That is sufficient enough," Wang Lei said, bowing his head.

He stood up and left the conference room without saying a word to anyone else. When he was gone, Benjamin turned his nose up like he smelled something foul.

"That motherfucka is racist!"

"What did you steal from his family?" Domino asked.

"A Van Cleef set," Benjamin said sheepishly. "I was about to resell it for a pretty penny."

"Well, I'd be racist toward your ass too!"

At first, Benjamin looked offended by Domino's words. He even went to respond, but nothing came out but a laugh. Soon they were all laughing together, even Niles, who was still sitting back. Damián patted Caesar on the shoulder.

"Good work, Caesar. I did not think this day would end so well."

"The Chinese still haven't agreed, so how well did it really go?" Caesar said, slightly disappointed.

"Four out of five families together isn't bad. And if Wang Lei tries to pull any funny shit, you'll have us to back you now."

"I just have one question though," Benjamin said, making another face. "You ain't really mean that when you said you wanted us to sign in blood . . . did you?"

I'm not a killer but don't push me.

Chapter 24

The Present

The kitchen of the Big House smelled deliciously of the bacon, waffles, and other goodies that covered the dining room table. Boogie was stuffing his face and laughing at Caesar's description of his grandfather. Caesar had suddenly stopped telling the story halfway into breakfast to answer a phone call.

"Is it time?" Caesar said into the phone. "Does Zo know? Okay."

Boogie continued eating his eggs and bacon while waiting for him to finish. He was truly intrigued by the history of the families. Moreso by the fact that Caesar was so young when everything took place. It was knowledge that he had already, but hearing it play-by-play was a history lesson he didn't know he needed. His hopes to hear the rest of the story were shot down when Caesar got up from the table and made like he was about to leave.

"Where you goin'?" Boogie asked and put his hands up in a confused fashion.

"I need to go meet with Zo."

"What about the rest of the story?"

"I'll have to finish another day."

"I thought the Chinese didn't agree to it at first. Didn't they try to fight you one last time?"

"They did, but that's nothing to waste too much breath on. They tried to go against me, but the others kept their word and stood beside me. Your grandfather was the main one to go toe-to-toe with them. Benjamin was a trip, I'll tell you that much. You remind me of him in some ways. But needless to say, Wang Lei knew he was fighting a losing battle and eventually joined us."

"That's it then?" Boogie asked and watched Caesar's eyes grow dark like they had earlier in the gym.

"Another day," Caesar said again.

Before Boogie could question him anymore, the pitter-patter of tiny feet could be heard a short distance away. Soon after, Amber came running into the kitchen with her cute morning face and hair all over her head. Once she saw Boogie, she ran to him and climbed into his lap.

"Dada?"

"Good morning, baby," he said and kissed her forehead. "You say hi to Uncle Caesar?"

Boogie pointed at Caesar, and Amber gave him the most precious wave with her little hand. Caesar returned her wave and made her showcase her six teeth in a bashful smile. She hurried to bury her face in Boogie's chest, and Caesar laughed.

"I swear I don't know how she learned to run that fast!" Roz's sweet voice filled the kitchen.

She entered dressed in a nightgown with a robe tied tightly over it. On her head she wore her green bonnet to protect the knotless braids she recently had installed. She seemed well rested and even had a glow about her that morning. Upon seeing Caesar, she kissed him on his cheek in greeting and went to the table to make herself a plate of food.

"I'm glad to see you in better spirits, young lady."

"Who, me?" Roz asked Caesar with a smile. "I guess you can say that. Amber is home, my man is safe and getting stronger every day. I'm a happy girl. And I'll be happier if this Negro doesn't kill himself in that gym."

Boogie almost choked on the piece of bacon he was chewing when Roz swung her head around to give him a death stare.

"What?" He feigned innocence. "Gym? I don't even know what that is."

"Yeah, all right. You're gonna be mad that you're playing with me when your ass hurts yourself and I don't come help."

"The two of you remind me of my wife and me when we were your age. Young, in love, and annoying to listen to!" Caesar laughed and gave them a wink before starting for the exit.

"Caesar, wait!" Boogie stopped him. "Is everything good with Zo?"

"Yes, there's nothing you need to worry your head about," Caesar told him with a blank expression. "I'll call you later to check on you. Remember what I said."

He left, and just Boogie, Roz, and Amber were left in the kitchen. Boogie made Amber a small plate and put her in her high chair so she could eat it. When he sat back down next to Roz, he pushed his own plate from in front of himself and tried not to let his thoughts run wild.

"What's wrong?" Roz asked while biting a strawberry.

"Nothin'."

"I don't believe you. Tell me what's on your mind."

"Caesar was lyin'. Somethin' is goin' on with Zo. He just didn't want to tell me."

"How do you know he was lying? He just told you that everything was fine."

"His face was too blank. He was tryin' too hard to not show emotion. Why would he do that if he weren't lyin'?"

"No idea, but you also could just be tripping. What did he mean when he told you to remember what he said?"

"Nothin'. Just that I should be usin' my downtime to spend with you and the baby."

"I couldn't agree with Caesar more! It's sad that it took us getting shot to spend this much quality time together."

"You knew what you were gettin' yourself into when you got with a street nigga," Boogie teased.

"I did," she admitted. "And that's why I need to cherish this time the three of us get to spend as a family before you jump right back in the game."

"I promise this time around I'm gon' be there more for you and Amber. Because if y'all aren't happy, then none of this shit is worth it." He leaned over and gave her a kiss. "Speakin' of happy, what's goin' on with you today? Why you glowin'?"

"Glowing? Me?" She seemed surprised by his question. Her hand went to her face and gently touched the side of it. "It must be my rosewater toner."

Boogie put the microscope on her. As he stared, he realized he'd been wrong. See, the thing about women was that they had the magical powers of hiding things in plain sight. You had to know what to look for. Her skin looked vibrant, and she had a smile on her face, but her eyes, they were the thing that couldn't lie.

"You been down to the cellar?"

"No, not yet."

"You want me to handle that for you?" Boogie asked, and she rolled her eyes.

"I don't need you to take out my trash. I got it."

"My bad. I was just makin' sure you're all right. He's been down there for days. He might be dead."

"Evil people like him know how to cling to life. I'm sure he's not dead, but that's how I want him. Clinging to life."

"Roz . . . are you *sure* you're gon' be able to handle the aftermath of all this?"

"I could say yes, and that might be a lie. But I could say no, and that could also be a lie. I won't know until the deed is done. How did you feel?"

"The first time I killed someone?"

"Yeah."

"Somethin'. I felt somethin'. I can't quite explain what it was, but I knew my life would never be the same after. It's somethin' you can't come back from. So if I can spare you that, I will. But I also know I have to respect you."

"Thank you, but I think I'll be fine." Roz let her eyes drift to Amber, who was busy stuffing her face. "He tried to kill her, baby. Look at her. She's the cutest and most innocent child I've ever seen, and he tried to end her life. Just so I couldn't have her. That thought has plagued my dreams every night. Even though I know she's home and safe with us, she almost wasn't.

"All Adam has ever done is cause me pain, and he thinks he's gonna come and continue to ruin my life? What he almost did to her, and what he actually did to you, is on me. The truth is I don't care who I become after. I just know that when I'm done with him, he'll be dead."

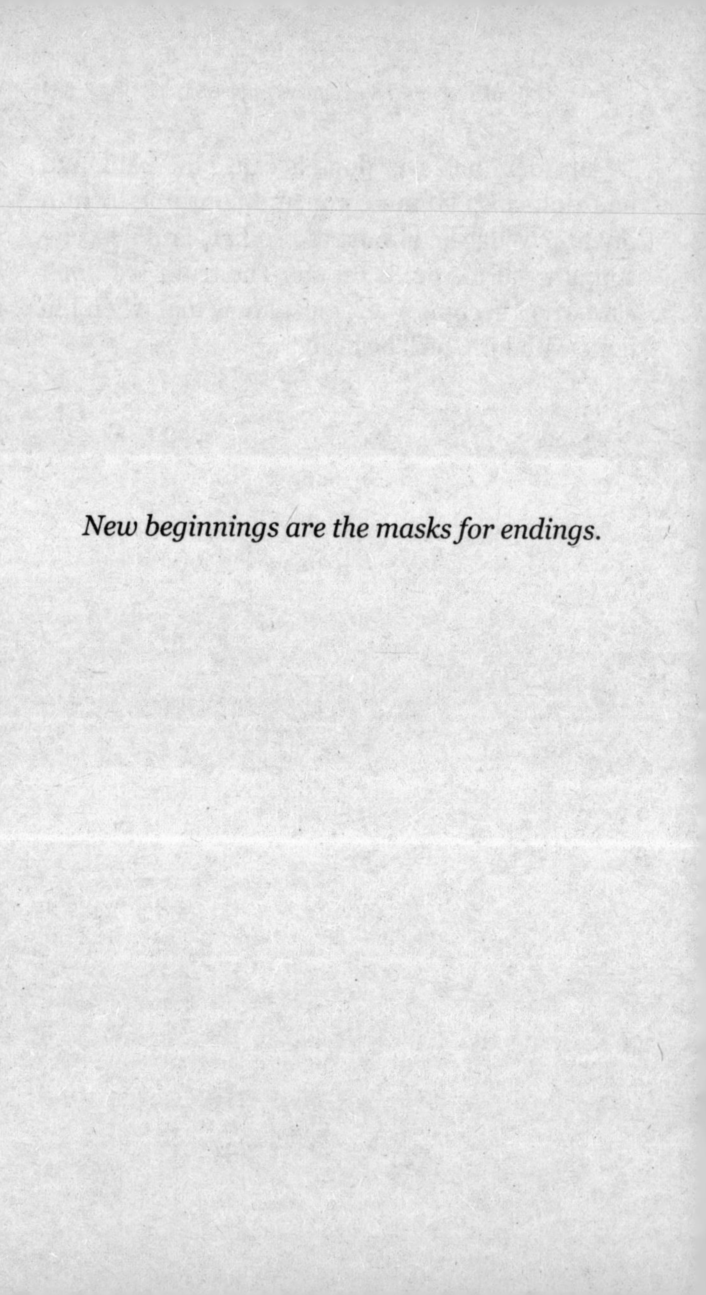

New beginnings are the masks for endings.

Always protect your heart.

Chapter 25

Later that evening, in a different part of town, Zo was busy examining himself in the hallway mirror of his family's home. He took a step back to get a better look. Fitted in a custom Prada suit, he was very dapper. He buttoned the jacket and made sure that the butt of his tucked pistol was neatly hidden away. He shuffled from foot to foot to make sure he was able to move comfortably with the blade he had strapped to his ankle. He was positive that he wouldn't need to use a weapon, but just in case, he was ready for whatever the night threw at him.

Zo contemplated meeting with Louisa all week, but he knew it was something he had to do. A part of him wanted to hunt her like a rabid dog and put her down. But even that seemed to be too kind. She deserved to have the same fate as him: to live a life of agony remembering what was lost.

"Lorenzo, I really think you should stay home tonight." His mother crept behind him and placed a hand on his shoulder.

Zo stared at her small frame through the mirror and saw that worry was written all over her face. It was for good reason. He was all she had left. If something happened to him, she might never recover.

"I have to go. If I don't, she might hurt someone else I love. And this time it might be you."

"But what if it's a trap? That bitch is evil, Lorenzo. You can't put anything past her!"

"I'll be fine, *Mamá*. I'll have enough men with me to ensure my safe return to you."

"Make sure of it. I won't forgive myself for letting you walk out that door if harm finds its way to you tonight."

Zo turned around to face her and pulled her into a tight bear hug. She buried her head into his chest and didn't let go until Rosaline stepped into the hallway. She was a woman about Christina's age and was dressed casually in jeans and a T-shirt. Although she was the help, she and Christina had developed a bond over the years, and Rosaline was allowed to dress comfortably for work.

"Mr. Alverez, everyone is outside waiting for you."

"Mr. Alverez?" Zo asked and raised a brow. "I must really be getting old."

"You are now the man of the house, so I will respect you as such," Rosaline said and stepped forward to fix his tie. "Don't keep your mother and me up waiting in worry, huh?"

"I will try not to."

"That's good enough for me."

"And please make sure she eats," Zo said, referring to Christina.

"I'll force it down her throat if I have to," Rosaline said and winked. "Come on, Christina. I fixed you some enchiladas."

"Lorenzo . . ." Christina gave Zo one last hug.

"I'll be back, *Mamá*. I promise."

He placed kisses on both of her cheeks, and she nodded tearfully. When Rosaline led her away, he let out a small breath of air and checked his appearance one more time. He wanted to look powerful. How had Marco done it all those years? All he had to do was walk into a room and everyone went silent. Zo had been told that his grandfather Damián had the same trait. Zo wanted to exude the same kind of energy to Louisa to embed in her head that she had messed with the wrong family.

He was adjusting the diamond ring on his pinky when his phone vibrated in his pocket. He pulled it out, quickly read the message on the screen, and placed it back in his pocket. It was time to go.

Outside, as Rosaline said, his men were waiting for him. He had no intention of being inconspicuous that night and would be taking three cars to the fish dock. Zo nodded his head at Tomás, the man holding his door, before he slid into the back seat of the Cullinan. Tomás joined him. He was an older man in his forties and had been loyal to Marco for years. He was a great strategist and a hell of a shot. If Zo was going into battle, Tomás was someone he wanted by his side. Even in light of recent events, his loyalty to the Alverez family didn't waver.

"*Estás bien?*" Tomás asked when the driver pulled away from the house.

"Do I not seem like it?"

"I am only asking because Marco's sister, this Louisa, seems to be even more of a shark than your father was."

"Then I guess it's time to shove a harpoon through her chest."

"What is it that you think she wants?"

"Me," Lorenzo stated. "Louisa wants to have me wrapped around her finger the same way my father was. She wants to pull our business from New York and wants us to work solely with her. I won't."

"I understand what you are saying, Lorenzo. But have you ever thought about the fact that she is an Alverez too? She had just as much right as Marco to the empire your grandfather built."

"And maybe that's why my father overcompensated her all these years. But that doesn't matter anymore. She killed my sister. There will be no coming back from that."

"What do you plan to do?"

"It's not what I plan to do. It's what has already been done."

Tomás gave Zo a quizzical look but didn't ask any more questions. Instead, he leaned back into his seat and rode with Zo in silence all the way to the fishing dock. The Blues fishing dock hadn't been used in years since the brothers who owned it died. However, someone must have been keeping up with it, because the dock itself looked to be freshly built. Even the warehouse right on the water seemed newly renovated with fresh blue and white paint. The inside was lit up, but Zo couldn't see much through the windows. He noticed cars parked on one side of the warehouse, and he instructed his driver to park in the same area. Zo and Tomás got out of the Cullinan followed by the ten men who were in the other two vehicles. Their weapons were brandished, and they marched behind Zo in a military fashion.

"The door is there." Tomás pointed at an open door on the warehouse. "They must be waiting for us."

"I hope so," Zo said, checking the Richard Mille on his wrist, "because we're late."

Tomás covered Zo's front as they walked into the warehouse, and the overwhelming smell of fish surrounded him. Standing in the center of the open floor of the warehouse, waiting for him, was Louisa. She was wearing a skintight black dress and high heels, and she rocked big, soft curls in her hair. And she was not alone. Around her stood at least twenty men all armed and waiting for her order. A smile crept to her face upon seeing her nephew and his men.

"Nephew! Don't you look nice in your little suit. Is that why you're late?"

"You're no family of mine," Zo told her, ignoring her question.

"Blood and genetics would state otherwise. I actually think we have the same eyes," she said in an amused fashion and then motioned to his men. "I thought you would bring more men with you."

"I see you *knew* to bring more with you."

"Oh, yes, I don't take these kinds of threats lightly."

"I'm glad you know that I'm a threat," Lorenzo growled.

"You on a regular day? No," she laughed. "But any man with the rage I've ignited in you is someone to watch out for. You're welcome for that. Daniella told me how you were struggling to fill your father's shoes. Hopefully I've helped with that."

"Don't you ever let me hear you say her name!"

"Who, Daniella?" Louisa taunted.

"I didn't come here to play games with you, Louisa."

"I know you didn't. You came here because you thought that if you didn't show, I would kill Christina. Which is true, so I'm glad you're here."

Zo breathed evenly, not letting on that the words were affecting him. He didn't want his anger to get the best of him. He could tell that was what she wanted. "What do you want from me?"

"The same thing I wanted before. For you to join me. Except now the conditions have changed."

"You and I both know that I'll never join you, so there isn't a point in me humoring you."

"Tsk, tsk. Lorenzo, how rude of you. You don't want to know what my new conditions are?"

"I don't give a fuck what they are, you psycho bitch!" Zo said, and she laughed loudly.

"Lorenzo, I'm your aunt. You shouldn't talk dirty to me. And although you didn't ask, I'm going to tell you my conditions anyway." Louisa clasped her hands behind her back and began pacing back and forth in front of her men. "I changed my mind about taking the operation from New York. It actually would be smarter to keep it here. There will be more money for me that way."

"More money for *you?*"

"Oh, yes. This is the best part, Lorenzo. You are going to step down as the head of the Alverez family, and I will take your place. You will work under me as a third in command, since as you know Nolan is already my right hand. Speaking of him, he should be here shortly to explain what your duties will be."

"Ha!" The laugh came from deep in Zo's belly. "See, this is how I know you're crazy. Because that will never happen."

"I don't think the decision should be left up to you. It should be left up to the Alverez family."

"You're talking about a vote?"

"Yes. I have just as much right to the throne as you if not more. Damián Alverez was my father, same as he was DeMarco's. And when Marco died, it should have come to me."

"*Abuelo* sent you away. If he wanted you to have any part of the business, he would have kept you around. We didn't even know about you."

"Hmm," Louisa chuckled. "You're right. And that caused so much pain inside my body. To not be wanted by my own father. Shunned by my own family. The same reasons why Daniella felt she could connect to me. That's why it was so easy for her to trust me. She thought I could understand her. And I tried, I really did. But the more I got to know her, the more I understood why DeMarco would rather it be you. See, me, I learned to stand up alone. But her? She was so needy! Always needing constant validation. '*Papá* loved Lorenzo more than me. *Papá* never saw me. Do you see me, *Tía?*' It was so annoying!"

"That's why you killed her, because she wanted love?"

"I've killed people for much less, trust me." Louisa shrugged.

"She was your family."

"Then why did killing her feel no different than killing a bug on the wall?" Louisa asked and feigned a curious face. "Anyhow, now you know my conditions. They are concrete and not subject to change. I've already infiltrated not only your operation but your colleague's as well. You've seen firsthand how far my reach can go. Abide and allow a vote to happen, or believe me when I say you will never get another good night's rest."

The answer to her request was easy.

"No," Zo said and gave her the coldest stare he could muster.

The ice from his gaze seemed to make her stop pacing. The smile frozen on her lips seemed to tremble at the corners. It was almost as if she were really thrown off by Zo's answer, and that shocked him.

"I hoped you wouldn't make this difficult. That offer was the last show of love in DeMarco's memory that I can give you, Lorenzo. I was trying to be fair, but now I will just take what I want! Enter!"

On her last shouted word, the doors behind Zo opened, and more armed men filed in, aiming their weapons. The only thing was they didn't have them pointed at Zo. They were pointed at Louisa. Zo wished he had a camera to capture the priceless look on her face when she saw that the small army of men wasn't hers. In fact, they weren't Zo's either. Zo grinned when the men parted and Caesar walked to the front of them.

"Am I late to the party?" he asked Zo, standing next to him.

"No, actually you're right on time." Zo grinned.

Zo's men advanced across the room toward Louisa's and forced them to disarm. Louisa watched with wide eyes as guns were placed to the heads of the people who were there to protect her. Anger took over soon after.

"What is this?" Louisa demanded to know. "Where are my men?"

"By now? Probably at the bottom of the river," Caesar answered her smoothly. "When Zo told me you wanted to meet him here, I thought it might be best that I tag along. People like you never seem to know how to do good business."

"But . . . how?" Louisa asked, clearly still dumbfounded.

"I knew you wanted to strike some sort of deal with me. But me being me, I would never agree to do business with you," Zo explained. It was his turn to be amused. "I also knew better than to trust that you would let me walk out of here alive when I refused you. Caesar here has known about this meeting all week. In fact, before I arrived this evening, he was watching you. And as you can see, he was able to ambush the ambush you had in place for me. That's actually why I was late. I was giving him time to handle his part."

Louisa's eyes had grown wide as reality was setting in. She'd been got at her own game. It didn't mend the hole she'd placed in his heart, but it still felt good. Zo gave his men the signal, and the sound of gunfire erupted around him. Louisa jumped out of the way as her men were riddled with bullets. When the last one dropped dead to the ground, she screamed in anguish.

"You stupid, stupid boy! You will pay for this!"

"No, I won't." Zo smiled and shook his head. "You won't get the opportunity to ever come at me again."

"Kill me and get it over with then," she sneered.

"No, death would be too much of a treat for you. I'm going to exile you from the state of New York and leave you to your agony."

"You're sending me back to my own kingdom as punishment? There is no agony in that."

"There will be when you realize that you are now truly alone," Zo told her.

Beside him, Caesar waved two of his men forward. Each was holding a burlap bag with fresh red blood seeping from the bottom. At the same time, they opened the bags and dumped the contents. Two severed heads hit the ground and rolled to Louisa's feet. Her mouth fell open, but no words came out. She was in utter shock as she looked down at them in horror. One of the heads belonged to Nolan. Along with his head being freshly severed, he had a bullet hole on the side of his forehead. That was enough to send her hand to her chest, but it was seeing who the other head belonged to that made her collapse to the ground.

"No!" She sobbed and crawled to the head that belonged to a young Mexican man. "Alejandro!"

"You made one grave mistake the last time you flew home," Caesar said. "You took Marco's private jet. The pilot informed Zo the moment you contacted him for travel. And Zo then told me. I took the liberty of beating you there and following you home. You led me right to your heart. He thought I worked for you when I told him that you had sent for him from New York. So sad, just another casualty of war."

She was sobbing on the ground next to Alejandro's severed head. Zo didn't think someone as evil as she was could even produce tears. It proved that she wasn't completely a demon.

"Now you know what true agony feels like. You killed my friend's child and tried to kill his last living one. You'll live with this pain forever knowing that your decisions led to your lover's death." Caesar spoke with no emotion. "Louisa Alverez, you are in the territory of the five families, where you will never show your face again. If you do, you'll be punished in ways that are much worse than death. You are now and forever exiled."

Face your fears.

Chapter 26

Roz wished she could blame her lack of sleep on Boogie's light snoring, but she couldn't. It was one of those sounds she had grown accustomed to, and she always slept like a baby when she was next to him. However, that night was different, and she knew exactly why that was. The thought of Adam being locked away in the cellar below them gnawed at the back of her mind. Three days had passed since anyone had gone down there. He hadn't been given any food or water and hadn't been allowed to use their restroom facilities. She had hoped that he would just die, but he was still holding on.

She glanced over at Boogie and then at Amber, who was snuggled underneath him. Careful not to wake them, she climbed out of bed and slid on a pair of jeans over her underwear. After throwing a hoodie on, she reached under the pillow, where Boogie always kept his gun. Since Amber often slept with them, he kept the magazine separate but next to the firearm, and she grabbed that, too.

Her footsteps were quiet on her way out of the room, and she looked quickly back at the bed before shutting the door behind her. She walked down the dimly lit hall and couldn't help admiring it. The floors were marble, and the lantern-style lights illuminated her way to the winding stairwell. Since her stay, she had fallen in love with the home and wished they could live there. However, she knew it was a safe house for all five families, not just her and Boogie. That was why he had it built so big. Still, she hoped as much detail would be put into their house.

Roz crept down the stairs and heard the sounds of a television coming from one of the sitting rooms closest to the foyer. Although there were people watching the exterior of the house, Boogie's cousin Tazz had made it his business to stay with them while Boogie was recovering. Once Roz reached the main level of the house, she inched alongside a wall and peeked around the corner to see into the sitting room. Tazz was there, but his consciousness wasn't. He was sound asleep on the couch in front of the television. An old episode of *Martin* was playing, and Roz saw Sheneneh pointing all in Gina's face.

Knowing the coast was clear, Roz went the rest of the way to the door that led to the cellar. It was biometric, and only a handful of people could get the door to open. She was one of them. Roz pressed her thumb against the keypad, and there was a low clicking sound when the door unlocked. When she swung it open, she flicked on the lights and took a deep breath. On her way down the stairs, she placed the loaded magazine in the pistol and tucked it away in the pocket of her hoodie. It was time to face her demons.

She stepped off the final stair and went directly to the cellar. There he was, still bound to the chair, staring at her as she approached. She began inhaling the strong stench of pee with every breath and turned her nose up in disgust when she stopped in front of him.

"You stink," Roz said and peeled the duct tape back from his lips.

"You would too if you were left in a cellar for this long," he said weakly. "Have you come to finally take me out of my misery?"

"Misery? I wanted you to be in despair. No . . . *torment*. Maybe I should leave you down here a few more days."

"No! Please. I'm begging you, just kill me."

"Now we're getting somewhere."

She looked at him in his frail state. She found it hard to believe the man before her was the same one who used to evoke such fear in her heart. He was just a mere shadow of him and barely even that. Still, Roz didn't feel sorry for him. In fact, she didn't feel like she'd put him through enough pain yet. To the right of her, there was a long counter against one of the walls. The cabinet had drawers filled with utensils. Knives to be exact. She walked over to one of the drawers and pulled a paring knife from it.

"Tell me something, Adam," she said with her back to him. "What was going through your head when you were about to smother my daughter to death?"

"I just wanted her to stop crying."

"Did it ever cross your mind that was because she didn't know you? That she wanted to come home to her mother?"

"I know that's exactly why she was crying."

"But you just couldn't bring her back to me, could you? Not the bitch who left you hanging while you were locked up, huh? Go ahead. You can let it all out. Speak your piece before I send you to hell."

"What happened to the two weeks?"

"I thought you were ready to die now," Roz taunted, turning to face him. "Plus, I just don't like the thought of you being this close to me."

"There was a time when you loved me being close to you."

"That was before the evil in you showed its ugly face. You getting locked away was the best thing that ever happened to me."

"Hmm." Adam gave a weak chuckle. "You know why I used to hurt you? It was just so *easy*. You were so weak, and I can tell nothing has changed. The only difference now is that you have a little knight in shining armor who makes you feel strong. But where is he now? Not here, and that's why you haven't done what you want to do with that knife yet. You're scared."

"I'm not scared of you."

"You'll always be scared of me. I'll always haunt your dreams. No matter what you do, I'll always be with you, and that's why you don't have it in you to kill me. Because you know it won't do a thing."

"It will. You'll be out of my and Amber's lives for good."

"Then do it! Do it, you stupid bitch! You've always been a stupid-ass cunt. You could never do anything right. And pretty soon Boogie is going to see that you aren't worth a damn thing! Just like I did."

His words made her angry. No, they infuriated her, so much that she charged at him with the knife aimed for his chest. Her hatred for him had such a hold of her that she hadn't seen him snap his wrists apart and break the zip tie binding them together. When she was close enough, he swung his fist with power and precision, locking in on her jaw and sending her flying backward. The knife in her hand went flying across the room, and while she was in a daze, Adam finished untying himself from the chair.

"A little trick I learned while I was in prison. Patience."

He stood up from the chair in his soiled clothes and took a step toward her. A slow, mischievous smile spread across his face, and she noticed a difference in him. Adam wasn't the feeble man he was when she had first come into the cellar. And by the way her jaw felt, he wasn't weak either.

"You were playing me," she said when the realization hit.

"Bingo. In jail there were times where I went whole weeks without food. And in doing so, I had to learn how to conserve my strength."

"You were waiting for me to come down here, weren't you?" Roz asked and tried to scoot away from him.

"Yes. I prayed every day that when you finally came back down here you would be alone. And it looks like my prayer was answered. Ironic, isn't it? You thought you were breaking me. But really it's me who's going to break you for good!"

He lunged at her and wrapped his hands around her throat. She felt her airway closing, and all she could see was the hatred in his red eyes. He bared his teeth, and she could see he was trying to use all his strength. Adam was going to kill her.

"N . . . no." She clawed at his hands, but there was no point.

"When I'm done with you, I'm going to go wake lover boy up and kill him, too. But not before he can see little Amber's dead body lying next to him. I can start over with a new family. One that appreciates me!"

He meant every word, and tears rolled down Roz's face as she choked for air. She fought, but he was just too strong for her body, especially with her energy waning by the second. She thought of the ones she loved the most in the world dying because of her mistakes and pushed them fast from her mind because she wasn't going to let it happen. She remembered the gun she had in her hoodie pocket and grabbed it with a shaky hand. When the room started to turn black, she used her remaining strength to put the gun to his temple. By the time Adam realized what was happening, Roz pulled the trigger.

The close range of the bullet entering his skull snapped his head to the side violently. His blood splattered on her face, and she shrieked. She felt his body grow limp on top of her, and she summoned any strength she had left to push him off. She made the mistake of looking into his dead eyes as he lay next to her, and she hurried to crawl away, gasping for air.

"Yo, Roz!" a voice shouted.

Shortly after, she felt someone's arms around her. She looked up and saw Tazz looking down at her. He had a stupid look of concern mixed with confusion on his face, and it almost made her laugh.

"He's dead," she said in a hoarse voice.

"Yeah, I see that." Tazz widened his eyes as he looked at Adam's dead body. "Why didn't you let me know you were comin' down here?"

"You were asleep."

Tazz looked at Adam and then at his bindings strewn on the floor. "How did he get free?"

"He preserved his strength and broke free. He . . . he was waiting for me. This whole time."

"Damn. Yo, Boogie would have killed me if somethin' happened to you!"

"Well, it didn't, and now the devil can get out of this house."

"Hell yeah. I'ma get that nigga out of here ASAP. We don't need that pissy motherfucka's blood fuckin' up the wine!" Tazz helped her to her feet and led her to the stairs.

She was able to lean her shaking body against him as they walked up the stairs. Roz didn't know if she was shaking because she had come so close to death, or because she had caused it. Maybe it was because her body was still regaining its strength. But either way, she was glad Adam was really gone.

Roz tried to think of a story she could tell Boogie as to why she had gone to the cellar alone, and so late at night for that matter. She would have to wake up early and put some makeup on her face because she was sure it would bruise up by the morning. But it looked like luck wasn't on her side with that.

The moment she and Tazz emerged from the cellar, the hall was brightly lit, and Boogie was standing at the door. He took one look at Roz and knew what had happened. Tazz instantly let her go and stepped to the side.

"Ay, I ain't have shit to do with this. I was in there asleep and watchin' *Martin* in my dreams. Gotta go!"

Roz stared in disbelief as Tazz made his quick getaway, leaving her to deal with Boogie's disappointment. They stared at each other for a short while, and she was waiting to hear whatever speech was about to come from his mouth. But he did something that surprised her in the moment. He embraced her tightly.

"Is it done?" he asked when he leaned back and looked down at her.

"Yes," she said into his chest.

"Then let it out."

He didn't need to ask her again. She clenched the back of his nightshirt in her hands and cried until she couldn't anymore. She cried for her past, for the present, and for the future she still got to have.

A wounded heart is always more dangerous than a wounded ego.

Chapter 27

While Boogie was out of commission, the last thing he needed to worry about was the money or the businesses. And Bentley was making sure of that. He always thought his job as the right-hand man was stressful, but filling in for the king surpassed the stresses of his regular duties. It wasn't just making sure that everybody paid their dues. It was keeping in contact with those who hired them for major heists and assigning the best people for the job, and *then* making sure those people paid their dues. It was guaranteeing that each of the businesses was running flawlessly and that the employees were taken care of. When a day was all said and done, he was beat. It gave Bentley a newfound respect for his friend.

That day was collection day. Before he could head over to Staten Island, he had one more stop in Brooklyn. He pulled in front of the apartment building and parked on the street. He instantly recognized the two guys standing by the stairs. Shotta and Deuce were Boogie's younger cousins and a fresh 20 years old. They were brothers but not twins. Shotta and Deuce's father was who some would call a rolling stone all the way up until he was paralyzed in a shoot-out gone wrong. Deuce was brown skinned while Shotta was light, and they both inherited their father's silky-smooth hair. Shotta wore his in a braided man bun on top of his head, and Deuce rocked long straight backs.

They were handsome young men and dressed like they were always ready to pose for the Gram. But the worst thing a person could do was judge them based on their exterior. They were hungry and would be the first to let anyone know that love and notoriety were the last things on their mind. Boogie recognized this in them and put them in position to eat. Not only did they watch one of Boogie's biggest stash spots, but they also reported the comings and goings on the block.

"Wassup, Bentley." Deuce was the first to greet Bentley when he approached them.

"Y'all good?" Bentley asked and slapped hands with both young men.

"Just bein' cool how we be cool. You know how it is."

"Fa sho. What's the word?"

"Everything is straight up there. Everybody been puttin' in that work on their jobs. Droppin' off that paper on time. Apartment 220 today."

"That's what I like to hear."

"Ay, Bentley man," Shotta said, rubbing his hands together, "when is my cuz gon' put us in on the real action?"

"Y'all not eatin' good standin' right here?"

"I mean, this shit is cool, but a nigga is ready for some *real* work. You know what I mean? Send me on a mission."

"You think you're ready for a big heist?"

"Is my last name Tolliver?"

"I don't know, nigga, is it?" Bentley asked and laughed. "You niggas could have your mama's last name or some shit."

"Chill yo!" Deuce laughed too. "But for real, son, I'm with my bro on this one. We're ready to make some real paper. Put in a good word for us to Boog."

"A'ight, little niggas. I'll think about it."

"Man, come on."

"That's the best I can do right now. Plus, everybody is a little tied up right now."

"Everything straight with cuz? We ain't seen him on the block in a little second." Shotta didn't try to hide the curiosity in his tone.

"Yeah, everything is good with bro. He's just tied up like I said. That's why I'm here handlin' business. I'm finna go up and safety the stash. All that shit better be there, too."

"'All that shit better be there, too,' head-ass nigga," Deuce mocked him.

"Ay, I'm the same head-ass nigga you're askin' for favors," Bentley reminded him before walking past them and into the complex.

He went up the stairs to the second floor and to apartment 220. Boogie's system with that stash spot was flawless. The apartment that the money was placed in rotated among four apartments inside the building. One was on top of the other on either side of the building. Hidden in the walls of each apartments was a chute in which money and guns could be sent up or down in case of a raid. When he walked in, the money was already waiting to be moved on the table in the dining room. He nodded his head in greeting to the men sitting on the couch smoking out of a back wood. Not having time to count the contents of the bag, he just scooped it up and left. He trusted Deuce and Shotta, so he was positive there wouldn't be an issue. They were loyal.

"I'ma see y'all next week," Bentley said to them when he reemerged from the building and headed to his car.

"Ay, Bentley! I almost forgot," Deuce called out when Bentley was tossing the money in the trunk.

"Wassup?"

"There was a motherfucka who came by here a few days ago lookin' for Boogie."

"He came here?" Bentley made a face. Nobody knew about the stash spot except the people who were supposed to know about it. "You knew him?"

"Hell nah. I ain't never seen the nigga before. He was just askin' about Boog."

"Did this nigga have a name?"

"Nazareth or some different kind of shit."

"Did he say what he wanted with Boogie?"

"Just that he needed to talk to him and get some business squared away."

"A'ight, well, you let me know if he comes back around here."

"No doubt."

Bentley got into his vehicle and drove away. He felt the hairs on the back of his neck standing up. He didn't like what he had heard one bit. Who was in Brooklyn asking for Boogie? It couldn't have been Louisa. Zo and Caesar had already handled that problem. But if not, then who? He had to push the thought out of his head for the time being or else it would drive him crazy. Plus, he was a firm believer that what was done in the dark would inevitably come to the light.

Bentley's last stop was on Staten Island. The meeting place was an old coat factory that was still in business. It was built in the sixties and was owned by Bosco's family. Some could call it the heart of the operation. It was the first business to ever wash their money. Now that Bosco was dead as well as his brother Eduardo, appointed to fill their shoes was Matteo, their younger brother.

Bentley didn't mind doing business with him. He wasn't power hungry like Bosco, stupid like Eduardo, or annoying like Stefano. He just liked business to run smoothly and stay running smoothly. Matteo had been trying to get in contact with Bentley for a couple of days, but he just had so much on his plate. They were finally able to set up a meeting time, and Bentley was just there to see what was so urgent.

He had to walk through the sales floor of the coat factory to get to the hallway that led to the offices in the back. At first, he was shocked that Matteo didn't have his normal muscle standing guard, but then Bentley got to Matteo's office door and understood why. The door was slightly ajar, and when Bentley looked inside, he saw Matteo with a fine young woman bent over his desk. The woman looked to be Italian as well with long, flowy hair and full, round breasts that jiggled with each of Matteo's strokes.

"Oh, Matteo. Keep fucking me just like that so I can cum all over your cock. Yes! Like that!"

Her moans seemed to get louder and louder. She was so fine that Bentley almost stepped to the side and let Matteo finish handling his business, but then he remembered time was of the essence. He banged his fist on the door twice to announce his presence. Startled by the noise, Matteo looked up and saw Bentley standing there. He smiled big and spread his arms in welcome as if his dick weren't still inside of the chick.

"Bentley! So glad you could make it!" His voice was cheerful, and Bentley looked away as he got himself together.

The woman rushed to throw her clothes back on and hurried out of the office with her head down. When Matteo was decent, Bentley stepped inside the room and shut the door behind him.

"Have a seat with me. We have business to discuss."

Matteo motioned to a seat across from him at his desk, and Bentley eyed it apprehensively. He didn't know what kind of freaky stuff Matteo was into. He examined the chair to make sure it was clear of any bodily fluids before he finally sat down.

"What did you need to meet with me for, Matteo?"

"I was actually hoping Boogie would be available, but he hasn't been returning my calls."

"He's wrapped up right now."

"I can understand that. But you are the next best thing," Matteo said and then grew silent.

Bentley watched as the cheerful expression on his face turned into a nervous one. Matteo kept opening his mouth to speak but then would stop right before any words could come out. Bentley watched him do it a few more times before he grew impatient.

"Look, man. I have shit to do. So let me know why I'm here."

"I'm sorry for my impotence. I just am trying to find the right words to tell you about the new problem we have."

"Problem?"

"Yes. See, there were things about the business side of things here on Staten Island that Boogie never knew about. And it never seemed important to tell him since he did away with everything my brother had put in place."

"Okay, so explain the problem."

"When Boogie took over Staten Island, he was under the impression that he was taking it from the Bertolli family, because we in fact have overseen the territory for years."

"You say 'overseen' like y'all were renting the shit or somethin'."

"You can say that. The Bertolli family were the face of the area. Although my father, Benzino, was truly the mob boss they say he was, he was just the underboss."

"And who was the big boss?" Bentley asked, his interest officially piqued.

"His name is Nasir Lucas. Years ago, when the pact was formed and Staten Island broke away from the other boroughs, he left."

"Why?"

"No clue. My dad handled things here for him, but Nasir called the shots. Some people called him the Grim Reaper. He was a minacious man with a powerful backing, just like the Kings and the Tollivers. When Nasir's son came of age, he started handling things hands-on in the island. And that continued up until the feuding started again."

"So you're telling me that Boogie thought he was takin' Bosco's territory, but really he was takin' it from somebody named Nasir?"

"Yes."

"And what has this Nasir had to say about it all? Because things have been real quiet around this way."

"They may not be for much longer, and that's why I called you here today. Nasir's son paid me a visit. And I have reason to believe he'll be looking for Boogie."

"His name doesn't happen to be Nazareth, does it?"

"What?" Matteo turned his face in confusion. "No. His name is Namir. And he's as ruthless as his father. Not to mention he's not happy about coming back to an empty well."

"Well, if he's lookin' for an issue, he'll find it fuckin' with Boogie. Choppin' down giants is what we do best."

"I hope so. I just thought it was best that I let you know." Matteo stood up to shake Bentley's hand in farewell but received a crazy look back.

"Now you know just like I know what I saw you doin' when I first got here. You need to wash them things!" Bentley shook his head and left the office.

He walked back out of the factory the same way he came and got in his car. As he pulled out of the parking garage, he called Boogie. When he didn't answer, he called again.

"Ay, I'm at this social security office gettin' shit squared away. Let me hit you back."

"Nah, fuck hittin' me back. Meet me at Big Wheels when you're done with that. It's important."

"Understood," Boogie said and disconnected.

Before Bentley put his phone away, he dialed Morgan's number. She answered on the first ring, and from the loud music in her background, he knew she was at the Sugar Trap.

"Hello?" she shouted into the phone.

"You busy?"

"Nah, I just had to drag this drunk bitch off the stage. This ho fell off the pole!"

"Sounds like you might be a little busy."

"Not really, just another day at the office. Hold on, let me go somewhere quieter." Bentley heard a lot of movement before the noise in her background was gone. "Okay, I'm back. But yeah, I'm still trying to show my mo . . . Diana that she didn't make the wrong choice by putting me in charge."

"You can call her Mom. That's what she is."

"You don't think it would be weird?"

"At first, yeah. But that's gon' pass. Y'all are bonded in a lot of different ways now."

"You're right. Then there's the fact that she did make me rich as fuck overnight."

"That's nothin' but love," he said, grinning in traffic. "I was callin' because I wanna spend some quality time with my baby. What you doin' tonight?"

"Apparently you," she answered seductively.

"That's what I like to hear. I'm meetin' with Boogie in a little bit. But after that I can order some food and be yours for the night."

"I like that. Let me know when you get home."

"Bet."

He got off the phone smiling, but it faded once he remembered there was a new enemy moving around town. For all Bentley knew, Namir had too much information on Boogie's operation. Especially if he found the stash spot. He wanted Boogie to hurry up with whatever he had going on because they needed to figure out the next play.

Don't get caught lacking.

Chapter 28

"Bryshon Tolliver, there are just a few things we need to clear up with you."

The voice belonged to Detective Scrotum. That wasn't his real name, but it was what Boogie was calling him in his head. His actual name was Detective Scott, and he was already getting on Boogie's last nerve. He didn't know if it was the messy brown hair or the freckles on his face that were annoying him. Maybe it was because he was staring at Boogie without blinking. Either way, Boogie was ready to leave.

Almost two weeks had passed since the incident with Adam. Boogie spent that precious time with his family and getting back to full strength. And whereas he wasn't back to 100 percent, he felt good. And that meant it was time to get back in the game. A part of it was clearing up the confusion that surrounded his supposed death.

When he walked into the social security office and told them who he was and what he wanted, they contacted the police. Two detectives showed up to take him to the precinct for questioning. Detectives Scott and Easley were talking to him to get his story straight. Boogie didn't like the way Scott was eyeing him down. It was like he was looking for a reason to put him in cuffs right then and there. It was obvious that he didn't trust Boogie, but that was okay because Boogie didn't trust him either.

"What do you need from me, Detective?"

"So if you're Bryshon Tolliver, who's the guy we put in the incinerator?" Scott asked.

"No idea." Boogie shrugged. "Because I'm alive and well."

"If that's the case, why are you just now trying to clear all of this up?"

"I didn't know that I was 'dead.' I only found out when paperwork was sent to one of my businesses saying that the ownership of it would be going to my estate." Boogie was lying through his teeth without batting an eye. "But as you can see, I'm alive, so there is no need for that. So if we could just get this cleared up . . ."

"Hm," Scott said, eyeing him suspiciously. "Weren't you injured?"

When he asked the question, Detective Easley leaned back in his chair and crossed his arms. As he leaned back, his head gave the tiniest jerk to the side. Boogie understood and shook his head at Scott.

"Nah, I wasn't."

"Now I know you're lying. We got the call about you on the radio saying that you'd been shot and taken to the hospital. *And* we got a positive ID on your body."

"Actually, Detective Scott, the call we got was about a young black male being shot, and this is New York. Black kids get shot every day," Easley butted in.

"Fine, you got me there. But it still doesn't explain the positive ID on the body. If it wasn't in fact Bryshon lying on that table dead, then why would someone say it was?"

"Drugs?" Boogie offered, and beside Scott, Easley tried to suppress a laugh. "Also, who is it you had ID my body?"

"It says here that it was a Jermaine Smith," Easley said, reading off the clipboard in his hands.

"I don't even know anybody named Jermaine Smith. If y'all just lettin' anybody come and ID bodies, ain't no tellin' how many people you accidentally have declared dead."

"So far, in my time here, there have only been two." Scott leaned forward and placed his arms on the table that separated him from Boogie. "You and Caesar King. Go figure. I'm not going to pretend to be naive here. I know the two of you are in cahoots in business dealings. And we know they aren't any good. Now, Caesar, he's good. We've been trying to bring him down since he was eighteen years old. The guy is bad news. And if you're wrapped up with him, I know you can't be any better."

"Is it because we're black?"

"Dammit!" Scott slammed his hands on the table. "This isn't a game."

"I don't think it is. You want to connect dots when there ain't shit to connect," Boogie said with his best poker face. "You're insinuating that I faked my death, but why would I do somethin' like that? It makes no sense. And if it was me who got shot and taken to the hospital, where's the record of it? I would have had to undergo surgery or somethin', right?"

"I checked into the hospital records already, Detective. There's no record of a surgery on a shooting victim that entire week."

"You hear your partner? Nothin'. So have the social security office fix my shit so I can go on about my life."

Boogie could tell that Scott was livid beyond words. His face had turned a beet red, and he had balled his hands into fists. It was probably Boogie's smug smile that was sending him over the edge.

"I don't think we need you for anything further, do we, Detective Scott?"

"No," Scott said through clenched teeth. "But I'll be watching you."

"Yeah, that's not creepy at all," Boogie told him and got up from his seat. "Can somebody give me a ride back to my car? Y'all did kind of kidnap me."

"I got it. I don't need my partner blowing a head gasket," Easley said and patted Scott on the shoulder.

Scott muttered something under his breath and stormed out of the room. Whatever outcome he'd been hoping for, he made it quite obvious that he didn't get it. Boogie and Easley left together and went outside to Easley's personal Dodge Charger. Boogie got in on the passenger side and adjusted the leather seat.

"You musta had a bitch in here or somethin'," Boogie noted, scooting the seat back to give his long legs some room.

"I had a date a few days ago with this fine black queen," Easley admitted as he drove away from the precinct.

"You? A black woman?" Boogie wouldn't have been able to predict that. Easley was the poster child white boy: blond hair, blue eyes, muscular. In fact, he looked like something straight out of *Baywatch*.

"That's all I date. I love the sistas."

"I wouldn't have guessed that at all."

"Why? Because I'm white?"

"Yeah, like white white," Boogie said and laughed.

"What does that mean?"

"It means it looks like you wake up happy every day and probably have a few boxes of Raisin Bran on top of the fridge."

"Fuck you, man," Michael said and then smiled. "And I love Raisin Bran."

"See! That shits hilarious as fuck. Funniest shit all day." Boogie had to laugh again. When he was able to control it, he grew serious. "And hey, Easley, thanks for the heads-up back there and tellin' me what to say."

"You can call me Michael, and don't mention it. You're important to Caesar, and that means you're important to me."

"I feel that. Caesar told me about how he and your old man were back in the day."

"My dad always tells me that he thought the day Caesar recruited him would be the worst day of his life. But it turned out to be the best. Caesar set him free."

"You say that like he was a slave or somethin'."

"Everyone is when you think about it. We're slaves to what's considered right and wrong, when really those things are based on situation and perception. My dad taught me that when I became a detective. That's when he told me the truth about everything. Like how we were able to afford to live so good off a detective's salary. I mean, we had a fucking beach house in California for crying out loud. I can't believe I didn't see it."

"How did you feel when you first found out?"

Michael grew quiet for a moment as he mulled over the question. Boogie didn't think it was that complicated of a question, but then again, maybe it was. Finding out your father was working for a drug kingpin was life altering. It was the kind of thing kids read about in books or watched in movies. It wasn't the kind of life most lived in real life.

"Honestly? I was okay with it. Before I made detective, I was on the police force, and I saw a lot of dirty shit being done for a lot less. If I were my father, I would have made the same decision, and when I finally was able to, I did. You and I aren't so different, Boogie. You have your hustle and I have mine."

To a lot of people, Michael would be considered a villain, but from where Boogie sat, he was a hero. When Caesar put him in contact with him, Boogie didn't think Michael would be so cool. But that was why nobody should judge a book by its cover. He knew right away that he could trust him, which was good because, by the looks of it, they would be hearing from each other often, especially with his partner riding Boogie's coattails.

When they reached the place where Boogie's Lamborghini was parked, he got out of the car. He gave a nod before Michael drove away. He was ready to go meet Bentley on Staten Island.

Normally he was very vigilant about his surroundings. But maybe he was eager, a little too eager, to be back in the game, because he didn't notice the all-black McLaren 720S parked a few spaces down. Or the person watching him from inside of it.

Stay dangerous.

Chapter 29

When Boogie pulled into the parking lot of Big Wheels, it was a regular day of business for the establishment. There were cars parked outside waiting to be serviced, and mechanics running around, grabbing the things they needed. He honked his horn in greeting, and they all waved enthusiastically when they saw it was him. Boogie spotted Bentley's car parked at the far end of the parking lot. He was standing outside and leaning on his car, waiting for Boogie. On his face was a pair of dark shades to shield his eyes from the sun. He also wore a pair of shorts and an open floral shirt.

"Ay, who the fuck do you think you are?" Boogie called out the window with a laugh.

"I been you for a hot second. I think I'm startin' to smell myself!" Bentley called back.

"Yeah, a'ight," Boogie said and parked next to him. He hopped out and dapped Bentley up before leaning on the BMW beside him.

"And I know you not over here talkin' 'bout me! This nigga came outside with the fresh Versace!" Bentley exclaimed, popping Boogie's collar.

"You know, the world ain't seen me for a minute. I was tryin'a get my Rico Suave shit on like you, but Roz wasn't havin' it."

"Ay, fuck you, a'ight?" Bentley laughed. "But fuck all that. You good? How's the shoulder?"

"Shoulderin'."

"Nigga, what does that even mean?"

"It means I'm good."

"A'ight, I'll take your word for it. It's good to have you back in these streets," Bentley told him.

"Hell yeah, it feels good to be back in 'em."

Boogie took a look around him at the familiar sight and gladly inhaled the scent of car shampoo. He missed things he didn't even know that he would ever miss. It was good being in his own neck of the woods.

"I ain't even gon' lie to you, Boog. It ain't easy bein' you. You made it look that way though. But this shit is a lot."

"Heavy is the head that wears the crown. Everybody wants that power, but nobody thinks about what kinda work it brings."

"Facts." Bentley made a "whew" sound and shook his head and then grew serious. "How's Roz doin'? She told me what happened with Adam."

"I don't know. She won't talk about it." Boogie shrugged. "She seems a'ight, but I know she's not. And if she really *is* okay, there's gon' come a time where she won't be. She's not a killer. And I'ma regret lettin' her do it for the rest of my life."

"Nah, I know my sister. She gon' be straight. And that was her cross to bear. Plus, I hate to say it, but with dealin' with a nigga like you and havin' somebody like me for a brother, that shit was bound to happen one day."

Bentley's words hit Boogie in the chest because he was right, no matter if he wanted to admit it or not.

"But anyway, let's get down to business. Did Caesar tell you what happened with Louisa?"

"He told me a little somethin' about it. He shoulda killed her though. Bitches like her never really know how to pipe down."

"I agree. I don't know what he was thinkin' by lettin' her go. If she comes back, we'll be ready."

"What else has been happenin' out here? I know you didn't call me here for that."

"Somethin' weird *did* happen. Somebody named Namir is out here lookin' for you."

"I don't know any Namir. You sure?"

"He showed up at the stash askin' Shotta and Deuce about your whereabouts."

Troubled, Boogie furrowed his brow. Nobody was supposed to know about that spot except for the people who needed to. Bentley's words put a sour taste in his mouth.

"Change the spot," he said.

"Already on it. I think I know why he's lookin' for you though. You know the setup we got goin' on Staten Island?"

"Yup."

"Matteo told me some interestin' things about the Bertolli family. Apparently, they weren't the ones really callin' the shots on Staten Island. Somebody named Nasir was."

"Nasir Lucas?"

"You know him?" Bentley asked.

"I know of him. Caesar told me a story about him."

"Well, this Namir dude is his son. And they aren't too happy about us takin' over their territory. Matteo said back in Nasir's day, he was considered a dangerous man."

"The Grim Reaper," Boogie said under his breath.

The befuddled look on Boogie's face showed how disturbed he was by the information, especially knowing that Namir had come to the stash house. He hadn't thought anything of taking over Staten Island because he had been so sure that the Italians were the only ones he needed to conquer. He tried to recall everything Caesar had told him about Nasir. He said that he worked with the Italians, not that he was the boss.

"Where these motherfuckas been at all this time?" he asked.

"No clue about Nasir, but Matteo said Namir has been off travelin' the world. He left Bosco in charge while he was on vacation."

"So I'm sure he was pissed when he came back and found out Bosco was dead. And that means I doubt he wants words with me."

"Hell nah!" Bentley agreed. "He's gon' move exactly how we would move if we were in his position."

"He wants me to die."

Boom! Boom! Boom! Boom!

The words were barely out of Boogie's mouth when the bullets from a high-caliber weapon rang out. He and Bentley jumped out of the way just as Bentley's car was hit by the gunfire. Boogie covered his head when the glass from the windshield fell from the sky like confetti, and he rushed to take cover behind the vehicle. He and Bentley met by the trunk of the BMW, guns drawn.

"They just shot my fuckin' car up!" Bentley shouted.

Boogie peered around the car just in time to see a black McLaren doubling back to send more shots their way. The passenger side window was rolled down, and Boogie could see two armed men in the car. He looked past the shooter and got a look at the driver's face. He didn't recognize the man at all. The passenger was out the window aiming an AR-12 at the BMW.

"Fuck this!" Bentley shouted and stood up.

If he was rocking, Boogie was rolling. He stood up as well, and the two of them began dumping bullets at the McLaren. The shooter was able to get a few more shots off, and Boogie felt them whiz past his face. However, he and Bentley were a much better shot than he was. Their bullets made his body jerk before he fell out of the car and onto the pavement. Leaving him there, the driver sped off fast, and Boogie shot at the car until his gun clicked.

"Fuck! He got away!" he shouted.

"But *he* didn't." Bentley pointed at the man on the ground.

He was still alive, but barely. He didn't look to be much older than them. His teeth were stained with his blood, and his breathing was labored. Even with that being said, he still managed to look up at them with humor in his eyes.

"Who are you?" Boogie asked.

"N . . ." The man tried to talk, but his breathing was labored. He coughed up blood and then tried again. "Namir is going to kill you for what you've done. There's nowhere you can hide."

Boom! Boom!

Bentley's gun sang out the last two bullets in its chamber, striking the man in his chest.

"Ain't nobody hidin', nigga." He spit on the dead body and turned his nose up.

There was noise behind him, and Boogie looked behind him to see what it was. Don Don, one of Big Wheels' mechanics, came running out of the garage to see what had happened. When he saw the dead body and the car, he didn't miss a beat.

"See, this is why we had to start offerin' pickup and drop-off services to our customers! 'Cause of shit like this!" Don Don shook his head and turned back to the garage. "Ay, Pee Wee! There's a body out here. And somebody come get Bentley's car in the garage. Goddamn, they fucked it up!"

"Don't remind me," Bentley huffed.

"Y'all go on and get outta here. We'll clean this shit up."

Boogie didn't need to be told more than once. He and Bentley got into his Lamborghini, which miraculously hadn't been struck in the shootout, and drove off. He was reeling with anger. It seemed like he couldn't get away from war no matter how hard he tried. But that was fine. It just made him stronger.

"What's the move, Boog? That shit can't fly." Bentley bounced in his seat, hitting his hand with his fist.

"I'm callin' an emergency meetin'. Now!"

Always play for keeps.

Chapter 30

One thing that Morgan had learned about her brother was that he was rarely in a bad mood. But when he was, it was a dangerous thing. And she knew he was in a bad mood when he called them all for an emergency meeting. Everyone had shown up and sat around the round meeting table. Caesar and Diana were there, too. They sat next to their old seats, which were now occupied by Morgan and Nicky. Boogie was in Barry's seat, Zo in Marco's seat, and Bentley sat in Li's seat, although he wasn't a family head.

If it had been a cartoon, they all would be able to see the steam coming off Boogie's body. He had his hands clasped tightly and pressed to his lips. His eyes stared at the table, and he looked like he was trying to calm himself down before he started talking. Nobody rushed him, even though they were all curious as to why they were there. Morgan especially wanted to know why Bentley had cancelled their date that night.

Things seemed to be going smoothly for everybody. And although Boogie had been injured, nobody she cared about had died, and that was a plus. Diana told her what had happened with Louisa, and her heart went out to Zo. Morgan felt that she didn't deserve to keep breathing, but Zo's punishment to her was worse than death. Still, she couldn't pretend to imagine what he was going through inside. She had an idea about it, but Boogie hadn't died when he got shot. Daniella did. And as selfish as it might sound, Morgan was happy that she wasn't the one feeling that kind of inward torture. But hopefully, one day, Zo would find some kind of peace.

"He shot at us," Boogie finally said in a low tone.

"Who? Who shot at you?" Diana asked, alarmed.

"Namir Lucas."

"Lucas?" she asked and looked wide-eyed at Caesar. "Isn't that . . ."

"Nasir Lucas's son," Caesar confirmed. He sighed. "I was afraid something like this would happen."

"You knew about him?" Bentley asked, wide-eyed. "He shot my car up. My *favorite* car!"

"I knew that the Lucas family played a part in the business that was conducted on Staten Island, but I thought it ended when I killed their boss."

"That's the thing. You didn't kill their boss," Boogie said, looking up from the table at Caesar. "You killed their employee."

"That doesn't make any sense. Nasir never had control on Staten Island. Back when my father was alive, he worked for Benzino. He didn't call the shots."

"And how sure are you about that? Because they didn't just shoot at us for no reason."

Caesar opened his mouth and then shut it again. His brow furrowed in vexation, and for once, he was speechless. He looked at Diana, who had a bewildered expression on her face. A chill went around the room, and a silence fell over them for a moment.

"I hate to say it, Boog, but you have got to be the unluckiest man in the universe right now," Zo spoke up. "But fuck it. We handled Louisa, and we can handle this new guy."

"But how? We don't even know where to find him. I didn't even know I had a new target on my back until today."

"Well, now you know," Morgan said. "And you know what he looks like."

"But once again, the question is, how are we going to find him?" Bentley reiterated.

"I think—" Diana started, but Morgan interrupted her.

"We flush him out. He should be looking for Boogie the same way Boogie is looking for him. Let's make it easier for him."

"And how do you suggest we do that?" Zo asked.

"Maybe—" Caesar started, but then Nicky interrupted *him*.

"Pass a message through one of the Italians. Set up a time and a place. Maybe there can be a peaceful resolve."

Boogie pondered Nicky's suggestion for a couple seconds before nodding his head.

"I like it," he said. "But this won't end in exile like it did with Louisa. I want his head. This is the last time I let somebody play with me. We haven't even been able to come together on the terms of a new pact. The fightin' has been back-to-back. I'm tired of this shit. I just got back on my feet. I'll be damned if I let a motherfucka take me off 'em again."

"I'm with whatever you're with, Boogie," Morgan told him, and everyone else agreed.

"I'ma make this call and let everybody know the move. Meetin' adjourned."

Boogie walked out of the high-rise building with Caesar at his side. Bentley and Morgan weren't too far behind them. The others had exited on other sides of the building. He still couldn't believe he had come so close to being taken off the map again.

Fed up was the only way to describe what he truly felt inside because that was what he was. Who would have thought the death of his father would have sent his world spiraling in such a way within a year? But then again, the only thing constant was change.

"Boog, I'ma ride with my shorty. Let me know what the word is," Bentley said and slapped hands with Boogie in farewell.

"Yup," Boogie said and then hugged his sister. "Keep him out of trouble."

"I should be saying that to you. Because of you, I'ma have to listen to him cry all night about how his precious car got shot up."

She kissed her brother on the cheek and took Bentley's hand. Boogie watched them walk away for a second before continuing to where his car was parked. He put his hands in the pockets of his shorts and turned to face Caesar.

"Why didn't you ever tell me that Nasir had a son?" he asked.

"Until I retold the story of how the five families came together, I honestly had forgotten all about Nasir. Our paths haven't crossed in decades."

"But didn't you want to do business with Bosco at one point? That's the reason you and my dad fell out."

"I did, but if I had known Nasir was still in the picture, I never would have tried to make that happen. And now that I know, I realize how much of a fool I was with Barry, my old friend."

"I thought you and Nasir were friends."

"Hm," Caesar said, and he seemed to go away for a second. "Maybe I should tell you the rest of the story now."

Revelations

Chapter 31

The Past

The sound of Earth, Wind & Fire filled the white room as Caesar and Amira danced along to the beat of "Serpentine Fire." He spun her around before pulling her close to him. When she was staring up at him with her bright eyes, he kissed her on her soft lips. She giggled and pulled away. It was her smile that always did it for him, and he was glad that it was back on her face. It took a little bit of wooing, but eventually a smooth-talking Caesar was able to get back into her good graces.

They continued to dance, and it was the first time since the death of his father that Caesar could say that he felt true happiness. Amira's light and energy was healing to him, and it was all that he needed to keep going. She had his full attention, so much so that he didn't even hear the music playing from the vinyl anymore.

"Your mother would turn over in her grave if she knew we were doing all this here in her precious white room!" Amira exclaimed, giggling again.

"No, I don't believe that at all. She would be happy for me that I found a woman as great as you to spend my life with."

"Life?" Amira stopped moving altogether and looked up into Caesar's face.

"You heard me. You're going to be my wife one day. Amira King has a nice ring to it, don't you think?"

"Yeah, but you don't feel like that's moving a little too fast?"

"I'm not talking about jumping the broom tomorrow. I'm just letting you know that I don't plan on letting you go anywhere. What we have is once-in-a-lifetime magic."

"I think so too. I've never loved someone like this before, Caesar. So if you hurt me—"

"I'm not going to hurt you, girl."

"Mm-hmm. Caesar, you're only eighteen. You're handsome and rich. I want this, I really do, but you have so much life ahead of you. And there are so many girls in the world."

"But the girl standing right here is just enough for me."

"And what about this?" She grabbed his hand and put it under her skirt. "Is this enough for you, too?"

"Hell yes."

She wasn't wearing any panties, and Caesar's hand fondled her love box. Parting her lips, he slid his middle finger up to her juicy clitoris and rubbed it in a gentle circular motion. He felt his manhood grow in his pants, and what he was planning to do to Amira on the couch might have been the thing to make his mother turn over in the grave. But just when he was about to pull his pants down, he heard the sound of someone clearing her throat. Caesar removed his hand and saw Martina standing in the doorway.

"You have a phone call. A Detective Easley," she told him.

"Thank you, Martina. I'll take it in here."

The phone in the white room was in the far right corner on a glass table. He picked up the receiver and waited for a second. When he heard a small click, he knew Martina had hung up in the kitchen.

"Detective?"

"Caesar, I—"

"I meant to call you and thank you for handling that for me," Caesar interrupted him, speaking about Damián. "Everything has been going smoothly since."

"Caesar, I need you to listen to me. They're coming." Easley's voice had a sense of urgency that made Caesar's blood run cold.

"Who's coming?"

"The Feds, Caesar."

"Okay, they aren't going to find shit."

"Are you sure? They got an anonymous tip about Cassius's death. The person knows for a fact that the gun that was used to kill Cassius is in your house! If they search and find it, you're going to prison for murder, Caesar. Do you understand me? Prison!"

"That's impossible! There isn't a gun here. The only way that could be is if somebody planted it, and nobody has been here to . . ." Caesar stopped talking when he realized Nasir was there two days prior. "Fuck."

He didn't know why Nasir would plant a gun in his house. He didn't even know if it was true, but Caesar refused to go to prison. He had to try to look. "How much time do I have?"

"They just left, so I'd say a good thirty minutes, give or take."

"Shit! Okay."

He hung up the phone and spun around the room. Where had Nasir gone while he was in the house? He couldn't have gone very far. It was just the white room. Amira was staring at him with a scared look on her face. He didn't have time to explain.

"I need you to help me look for something without making it look like we were in here looking for something."

"Caesar, I don't understand."

"Amira, please. Listen to me." He went over to her and placed his hands on her shoulders. "It's important."

"Okay." She nodded. "Okay. What am I looking for?"

"A gun. And we need to find it fast."

"Okay."

She didn't ask any more questions. She rushed to a couch and started looking in the cushions. Caesar went and did the same with the other. Nothing. They searched every nook and cranny in the white room and came up with nothing. By the time they finished, a good fifteen minutes had passed.

"Where the fuck could it be?" Caesar put his hands to his head and tried to think. Then he remembered Donald was the one who let him in. "Donald!"

"Yes, sir?" The butler appeared in the white room quickly when he heard how urgently Caesar called his name.

"When you let Nasir in the other day, did he do anything suspicious?" Caesar asked and watched Donald rack his mind.

"Actually . . . yes. He did. When I went back to get him and bring him to the white room, he wasn't by the front door where I left him. He was standing by your father's fish tank in the main living room.

How he ended up there and why, I don't know. I, for one, always thought that thing was a waste of money. He didn't even like fish . . . Wait, where are you going?"

Caesar ignored Donald's question as he rushed past the old man and to the living room. The fish tank he spoke of was huge and against the wall. The fact was the King mansion was so big that most of the rooms didn't get used often, and that living room was one of them. However, it was the room closest to the front door, and if Nasir was trying to hurry up and plant something, it would make sense that he put it there. The tank was heavy to move, and Nasir probably didn't have time to move it to hide anything behind it, but he could have tossed it.

Getting on the ground, Caesar looked under the fish tank and could make out something behind it. He forced his arm under the tank and reached as far as he could, feeling around with his hand. Finally, the tips of his fingers touched something, and he was able to get just enough grip on it to pull it back. When his arm was free and he was able to look down at his find, his jaw got tight. It was a gun, one he'd never seen before and one that didn't belong there. And by him grabbing it, it now had his fingerprints on it.

"You found it!" Amira's voice sounded behind him.

Caesar grabbed the gun and stood up. There wasn't much time left, and he didn't want to chance hiding the gun somewhere else in the house. Knowing how badly the Feds probably wanted to take him down, there was no telling how extensive a search they would do.

"Baby, the Feds are coming here to look for this. I need you to take it to Niles. He'll get rid of it."

He half expected Amira to tell him no and that she didn't want any part of what he had going on. But she surprised him by taking the gun from him and nodding her head.

"I'll take one of the cars and leave out the back gate," she told him. "I'll be back before you know it."

As she ran to the back of the house holding the gun in her hands like a fragile baby, Caesar knew. That was when he knew for certain that she was going to be his wife.

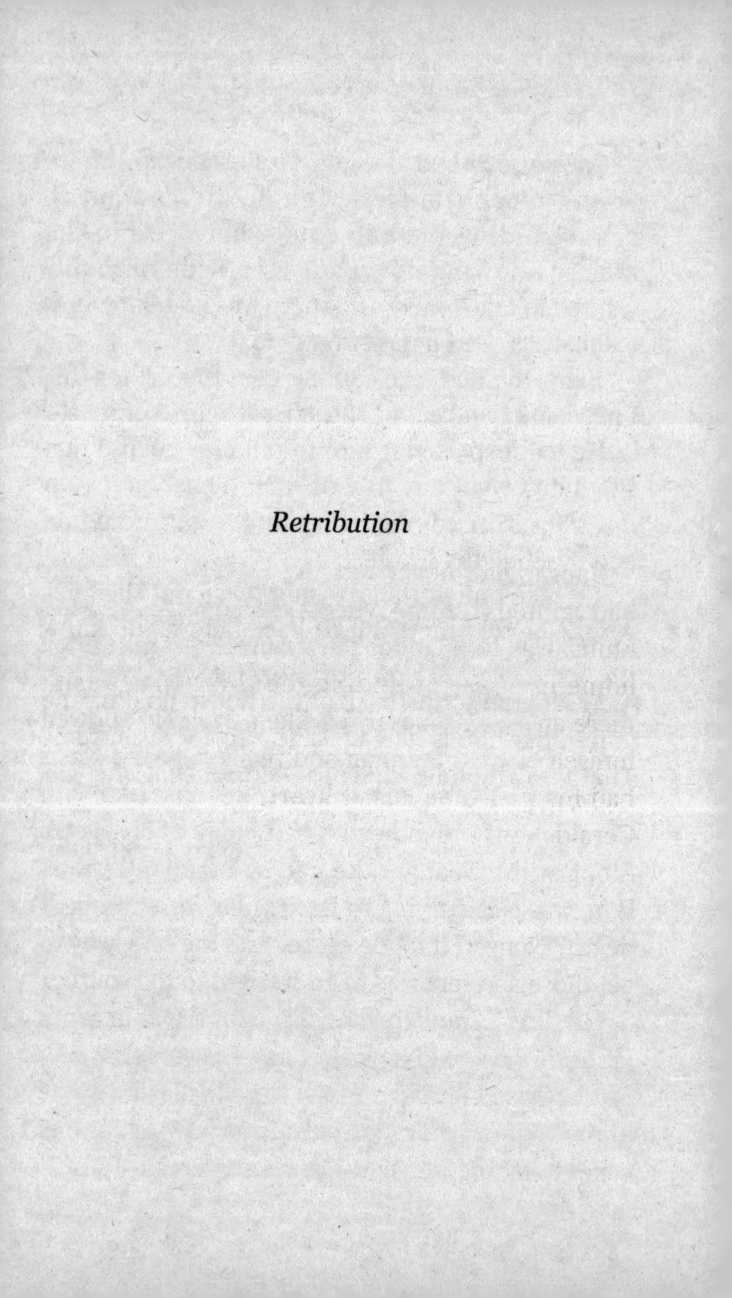

Retribution

Chapter 32

The Past

Caesar had never felt the kind of fury Nasir had ignited in him. When the Feds finally came, Amira was long gone. They ransacked his entire home in hopes of finding the thing that wasn't there anymore. Caesar felt like a fool. He allowed himself to trust the man and really believed Nasir had his best interests at heart. But just like with Gerald, Caesar had been a bad judge of character. Along with the anger, he had so many questions. *Why* was Nasir trying to frame him with Cassius's death? None of it made sense. And the only way to get those answers was to go straight to the source.

He didn't want to show up with a whole army. He knew he would never get any answers that way. But he wasn't stupid enough to go to Nasir's home alone. Niles accompanied him and was just as eager to figure out what Nasir's angle was.

"When you think about it, there's no way to justify what he did," Niles said as they neared Nasir's mansion. "He's the enemy."

"I know. I just want to know why he did it," Caesar said. "He and my father did good business together."

"Exactly. He did good business with *Cassius,* and now that he's gone, he probably wants the whole pie to himself."

If that was the truth, Nasir could have just killed him. There had to have been more to the story than just that. When Caesar pulled the car up to Nasir's house, there were more Italian men than last time waiting outside. It felt to Caesar like they were waiting for him.

"You sure you wanna do this?" Niles asked, eyeing the guns in their hands.

"Yeah. This motherfucka tried to send me up the river. Let's go."

The two men got out of the car and approached the front door. The Italians moved in front of it, forcing them to stop.

"Tell Nasir I'm here to see him," Caesar said.

"No need. He's waiting for you already," one of the men said and opened the door.

"You must have just wanted to say that. Why did y'all even move in front of the door in the first place?" Niles asked. "Just stupid."

"What's stupid is you being foolish enough to come here. Your funerals though."

They laughed and closed the front door when the two men were inside. There were more Italian men standing in the foyer of the mansion waiting for them to enter so they could disarm them.

"Get your fuckin' hands off me! I don't swing that way!" Niles shouted as they restrained him.

Caesar, on the other hand, was calm. He let them find and take all his weapons without fighting. Once they were done, Caesar and Niles were led to the same office in which Caesar had first met Nasir. He was seated at his desk wearing a nice suit and puffing a cigar. The sun filled the office with natural light as it shone through the window. Nasir didn't bat an eye when Caesar and Niles were thrown into the room.

"It's good to see you again, Caesar. I was expecting you yesterday, but today is as good a day as any. Take a seat," Nasir instructed.

"We're good where we're at," Niles told him.

"I wasn't giving you a choice."

He leered at the two of them as they slowly sat down. The only thing about Nasir that was the same to Caesar was his looks, but everything else had changed. The energy around him seemed dark, and the way he spoke was ominous. Caesar couldn't see his father willingly doing business with a man like that. He wouldn't have trusted him.

And neither would have Caesar had all the colors been shown.

"I guess I don't need to ask you if you did it, do I?" Caesar asked.

"Plant the gun? Yes."

"Why?"

"You came all this way to ask that simple question?" Nasir laughed. "It's a question you can answer yourself, really. You're smart. You can figure it out."

"Humor me."

"Fine," Nasir sighed in a bored fashion. "Your father, Cassius, and I did good business together. Great business, but the truth is I never really told him the truth. You see, I have a problem with not putting all my cards on the table. I don't like people to see everything in my hand. I have my own plans, and unfortunately your father's plans were getting in the way of them. I couldn't have him getting all high and mighty on me before I could really get into position. If he had control over each borough, how would I ever be able to kill him?"

"Kill him? You didn't kill him. Ed and Joseph did!" Niles exclaimed.

"No, don't you see, Niles? He set it all up," Caesar said, not taking his eyes off Nasir. "Didn't you?"

"Guilty." Nasir grinned devilishly. "But in my defense, Ed and Joseph were already halfway out the door. I just gave them the final nudge.

There's nothing like murder without getting your own hands dirty. I wish I had been there though. I would have loved to see the giant fall from the beanstalk."

Caesar could tell that he was trying to get a rise out of him, and he was. Caesar's blood was boiling at a dangerous temperature, but he kept his face calm. Nasir had already taken enough from him. He refused to give him any more.

"And once he was dead, you needed me out of the way next."

"Ding, ding, ding! But see, I couldn't just kill you. I have a detective in the borough, and I was just trying to throw them a bone. It would have been a win-win for everyone. I should have known you would be crafty enough to have a few in your pocket as well. You should have just taken that way out. Now I have to take your soul."

From under the desk, Nasir brandished a gun and pointed it between the two of them. He gave Caesar a sickening smile and then slowly pointed it at Niles. Niles, who had never been a man to show fear in the face of death, stared down the barrel of the gun, ready to part with the earth.

"I thought it was me who you wanted," Caesar said as Nasir fingered the trigger.

"It is, but before I kill you, I want to see the look on your face when he dies. I can tell you're very close."

Nasir squeezed the trigger on the word "close" and sent a bullet whizzing past Niles's head, shattering a statue. He shot the gun again, that time lodging a bullet in the wall. Niles flinched at the second shot, and there was joy in Nasir's eyes. He was playing with him. Caesar knew then that it was time for *him* to stop playing with Nasir.

"You said earlier that you don't like to let people know all the cards you hold? Well, neither do I," Caesar said, allowing a slow smile to come to his face. He could tell his sudden change in demeanor got Nasir's attention. "I kind of figured you had something to do with my father's death when I found the gun, but I still needed to hear you say it. Now you can die."

"How are you going to kill me when I'm the one with the gun?"

"I never said I was going to be the one to kill you," Caesar said and pointed at Nasir's chest.

Nasir glanced down at the collared shirt under his jacket to see a red dot dancing there. His eyes widened, and he tried to jump out of the way before the shot came. He managed to move to the left seconds before the window shattered from the gunshot, but he still got hit in the shoulder. When he fell to the ground in agony, Niles jumped into action and grabbed the pistol from Nasir's hand.

"Now who's got the gun, sucka?" Niles said, aiming the weapon at his head.

More gunshots could be heard outside the office as a fight ensued. They were getting closer and closer, but Caesar didn't budge.

"What's going on?"

"Right now, your men are being slaughtered like cattle," Caesar told him. "And as far as you, I don't know if that was Damián who shot you. Or it could have been Benjamin, maybe even Domino."

"What are you talking about? Those are—"

"The heads of the most powerful families in New York. I know. I did something that neither you nor my father ever could. I formed an alliance with them, and now going against me is going against them. Surprise."

"No." Nasir shook his head.

He used his good shoulder to scoot backward toward the bookshelf on the wall. Caesar was enjoying watching him look so weak. Nasir's biggest mistake would forever be underestimating him.

"Kill him," Caesar instructed.

Niles went to pull the trigger, but the office door swung open, and an Italian man stumbled through. He was holding a gun in one hand and clutching his stomach, trying to stop blood from leaking out. He was clearly badly injured, but that didn't stop him from defending Nasir. He shot wild shots at both Caesar and Niles, forcing them to take cover. Niles switched targets and shot the Italian in his face. Caesar scrambled back to his feet just in time to see Nasir escaping into a secret passage behind the bookshelf.

"No!" he shouted and tried to make it to him before he closed the bookshelf.

"Better luck next time." Nasir winked and slammed the bookshelf shut.

"You bastard!" Caesar shouted. "If you ever show your face anywhere in New York again, I will kill you! Do you hear me? Everyone will have orders to kill you on sight!"

War

Chapter 33

The Present

When the story was finally over, Boogie was shocked to learn that Nasir had been the enemy all along. He also felt like he understood Caesar more than he ever had. They both lost their parents at young ages and had to take over empires before they were ready to. It made sense why Caesar took him under his wing. It was more than him being Caesar's godson.

"You must see a lot of you in me, huh?" Boogie asked, and Caesar nodded.

"I do. And I've tried to spare you a lot of emotions that come with the losses."

"And I appreciate you for that. I'm sorry about your wife. She seemed like a real ride or die."

"She was." Caesar smiled fondly. "But she died peacefully, and that's the best way I could have hoped to see her go. I can't wait to be with her again. One day."

There was a deep longing in his voice, and Boogie noticed it. He understood. He would be ready to go too if Roz were no longer part of the living. He wouldn't want to continue without the love of his life. He couldn't. Caesar was a strong man for being able to do so.

"You're a good man, Caesar. If I grow up to be like you, I wouldn't be mad," Boogie told him and then pointed his thumb at his car. "You need a ride to your whip?"

"I'll manage."

"A'ight, I offered. I'm about to get out of here. I need to make them calls I—"

He couldn't finish his sentence because Caesar embraced him tightly in a fatherly hug. At first, Boogie was tense in shock, but then he hugged him back. It didn't last long, but it was healing. Boogie didn't even know he needed it.

"I wanted to do that when I first got back into the country," Caesar told him when he pulled away, "when I saw you on that couch after thinking you were dead. I probably hid it well, but seeing you like that about did it for me. Sometimes I wish I hadn't gotten so close to you or the others. I'm afraid to lose any of you. It would be the straw that broke this big-ass camel's back."

Boogie opened his mouth to respond, but the sound of clapping coming from an alley stopped him. Both he and Caesar turned and looked at the darkness curiously to see who was clapping. The person stepped out of the shadows, revealing that it was a black man around the same age as Caesar. He was bald too, but much skinnier. He had a look in his eyes that instantly made Boogie think of death because of how cold they were.

"Well, isn't that so sweet," he said.

"Nasir," Caesar sneered.

"I truly enjoyed that rendition of the story. I've only heard it from my point of view."

"You aren't supposed to be here."

Nasir looked to his left and then to his right before shrugging his shoulders. "I don't see anyone here who can stop me," he said. He grinned when both Caesar and Boogie went for the guns on their hips. "Tsk, tsk. Don't you think I thought of that?"

Two darts shot from the alley directly at Caesar and Boogie. It happened too fast, and they weren't able to dodge them. Boogie was hit in the neck and instantly got sleepy. The last thing he saw as he was collapsing to the ground was Nasir waving his hand.

"Mmghh . . ."

The moan that escaped Boogie's lips signified that he was regaining consciousness. He clenched his eyes shut before opening them. It didn't help. His sight was still blurry, and not only that, but his head was throbbing like someone had knocked him over the head. He was lying on his side on a marble floor and went to rub his eyes to clear his vision but found that he couldn't. They were tied together behind his back. He squinted down at his ankles and could make out red zip ties on them. He assumed that was what bound his wrists behind his back. Slowly, as his eyes began to focus, his memory started to come back to him. And then it hit him. He'd been kidnapped. Not only that, but he was alone. What had been done to Caesar?

He looked around at the large building he was in. It wasn't a warehouse. By the infrastructure, it looked like it used to be a reputable place of business. He was by himself in the middle of a huge floor space. His grunts echoed as he sat himself upright to get a better look at the place. The floor-to-ceiling windows had long drapes over them, and the walls had square light sooty stains on them. The stains let him know that photos had once hung there. At one point it had to have been some sort of art studio. The rats running along the wall told him it hadn't been occupied in quite a while.

Suddenly, Boogie began to hear footsteps nearing him. The room he was in was shaped like a pentagon, and every side led to a hallway. Because of the echo, he couldn't pinpoint which way the footsteps were coming from.

"I was starting to think that I would need to pour a bucket of water over you to get you to wake up."

The smooth voice came from a hallway on his right, and Boogie jerked his head toward it. The person who materialized was the same man Boogie had seen driving the McLaren earlier that day. He stood six feet tall and had a young face but very old-looking eyes, like they'd seen a lot of horror in their time. He wore a peanut butter–colored tailored suit that went well with his dark skin. The hair on top of his head was set in sponge curls, and he had a goatee. Boogie looked behind him and saw that he was alone.

"Namir," Boogie said.

"They say you know you've made something of yourself when people know who you are without you telling them," Namir told him with the hint of a smile.

"Where's Caesar?"

Namir didn't answer at first. Instead, he began to walk around Boogie. His hungry gaze never left Boogie. He was like a hungry tiger circling its prey. Boogie turned his head so that he could see Namir at all times.

"Caesar?" Namir finally spoke. "He's with my father having a good ol' time. They're old friends, I heard."

"What do you want?"

"Don't ask stupid questions. I can tell by how you run your business that you're a smart man. I've been following your people, waiting for you to resurface. If we had met on different terms, I'm sure things would have been much different than they are. But as you can see, they aren't. You owe me a lot of money, Boogie."

"I don't owe you shit!"

"Oh, but you do. You see, I had the perfect system going. My father put me in charge, and everything was great. So great that I decided to travel the world while Bosco ran things for me. There's no point in being the boss if you can't enjoy the fruits of your own labor, am I right? But then, you and Caesar thought it was okay to just send my whole operation crashing down. See, you started robbing me the moment you set up shop on Staten Island. The second money started going into your pocket, it stopped going into mine. It's not something I take lightly."

"You shouldn't have left your kingdom so wide open. And you trusted Bosco to keep things runnin' for you? That motherfucka was powerin' up. He almost got into business with another kingpin, but we killed him, too. I don't know, Namir. Maybe bein' a boss ain't your thing. You kinda suck at it."

"Augh!" Namir's angry shout was followed by him kicking Boogie in the face.

Boogie fell to the side and tasted the blood from his busted lip. He laughed through his grimace. He figured that would be Namir's reaction. Most people hated when mirrors were put to their faces.

"Can't handle the truth, can you?" he panted and put himself upright again. "You know what I think is really happenin'? Daddy put that pressure on you because you fucked up. And now you're doin' whatever to get back in his good graces."

"Maybe you're right." Namir knelt in front of him. "And that could also be the reason I'm going to kill you instead of just making you pay me back the money. Because you know what's priceless? Your soul."

He pulled a SIG from his waist and put it to Boogie's temple. Boogie knew that in his profession he was subject to death at any time. However, after that last near-death experience, he realized how much he wanted to live and how much he had to live for. Amber's face came to his mind, and his heart filled with a powerful will. She needed him. When Namir put his finger on the trigger, Boogie laughed in his face to taunt him.

"You're weak. You gon' kill me like this? Can't even fight me like a man."

Namir seemed taken aback by his words. He lowered the gun for a moment, and it seemed as though he was rethinking the manner in which Boogie would die. But then he smirked and put the gun back to Boogie's temple.

"This isn't a fucking movie. And I'm not going to chance you whooping my ass. I think I'll kill you this way. Say your prayers."

Boogie closed his eyes, not wanting his last sight to be of Namir's evil gaze. He thought of his family. Of Roz, Amber, and Bentley. Morgan and Diana. Tazz, Zo, and Nicky. He smiled, hoping they all knew what they meant to him. His only regret was not being able to say goodbye.

Boom!

Final Goodbyes

Chapter 34

A painful blow to the gut jarred Caesar awake from his dreamless sleep. One minute he was standing outside with Boogie, and the next he was in what looked like a dimly lit conference room. He doubled over and spat blood on the floor. A fit of coughing came over him, but when it was over, he sat back upright and could see that he wasn't alone.

Nasir stood before him. Minus the fact that he clearly had aged, he was still the same man Caesar had met all those years ago. He didn't bother to hide the brooding energy around him. Next to him, cracking his knuckles, was a young, muscly man. They both leered at Caesar like he was the scum on the bottom of their shoes. Caesar wasn't bound to his seat, but he was weak. Whatever kind of tranquilizer had been used to knock him out was still in his system, making him feel woozy. He blinked to clear his periodic double vision and focused on Nasir.

"Glad you could join us," Nasir said. "I'm sure you're feeling the effects of the horse tranquilizer we shot you with. So no need to tie you up."

"Where's . . . where's Boogie?"

"Somewhere experiencing bliss," Nasir answered. "Well, bliss for my son. And hopefully terrible, terrible pain for Boogie. He made a mistake, and now he has to pay for it. And you? You've had this coming for decades. I've dreamt of this moment."

"I won't . . ." Caesar caught his breath before speaking again. "I won't comment on how strange it is that you've had dreams about me for decades. But that hate must be what's kept you young all this time."

Nasir nodded his head at the young man, who gut punched Caesar again.

Caesar's shout filled the room. He sucked in a deep breath and exhaled it, trying to eat the pain. He forced a laugh and looked at Nasir. "Okay, I lied. You look like shit. All these years in exile haven't been good for you."

"Exile? I have moved in and out of Staten Island for years. When I learned fully of the pact you made with the other families, I was sure you wouldn't allow the Italians in the fold."

"They chose not to come. And I was fine with that. Benzino was too loyal to you. Now I know why. He was your lap dog."

"Real power lies in the one nobody is expecting. It's patient and always waiting for the right time to strike."

"I bet I can guess your plan because I'm sure it hasn't changed in all these years. First, you kill me to showcase this power. And then, you take over?"

Nasir didn't honor him with a response. He paced back and forth in front of Caesar a few times, chuckling to himself. When he finally stopped and faced Caesar, he emitted a long sigh.

"Don't you recognize this place?" Nasir asked and motioned his hands around the room. "You should know it like the back of your hand since you visited so much as a kid. Cassius said your mother used to bring you *all* the time."

Caesar's brow furrowed, and he surveyed the room thoroughly. The walls were dirty, and he was almost positive there was mold in one of the corners, but there was one painting on the wall that stood out. *The Saxophone Man*. Nasir had brought him to what used to be The Museum of Fine Black Arts. It had closed due to the toxic mold growing inside the walls. Caesar used to promise himself that he was going to buy the building and revamp it, but as the years passed, it became but a distant memory. They weren't just in the museum. They were in the exact room that Caesar brought the five families together in. It would have been a great nostalgic moment if the predicament were different.

"Ahh, you do remember," Nasir said, watching the recollection come to Caesar.

"Why did you bring us here?"

"Your humble beginnings were here. I figured there was no better place to end you," Nasir told him. "You asked what my plan is. The truth is, I don't want the same things that I used to. I've been content living my life quietly and handling things remotely through my son. I don't care to rule over this domain anymore. But the pride in me just can't let you do it either. So that's why I want you dead."

"That's stupid," Caesar told him bluntly and ignited a look of rage on Nasir's face.

"You know what my biggest mistake was the last time we were face-to-face? I talked too much," Nasir spit out and waved his nephew forward. "James, beat this motherfucka until he falls out of the chair, and then beat him into the ground. When we dump his body outside his gate, I don't want him recognizable."

James didn't need to be asked again. He stepped forward and commenced beating the living daylights out of Caesar while Nasir watched. The blows from the man half his age hurt like hell, but Caesar didn't once beg him to stop. He blocked what he could block, but eventually, he was beaten out of the chair. The man's size-eleven boots found their way to Caesar's body, and the elder man curled up with his head tucked. Never in his life had he taken an ass whooping like that one, and whenever he thought it was over, another blow came.

When finally they stopped, Caesar breathed heavily. He struggled to pull himself up on shaky arms, but finally he made it to a sitting position. Blood from a gash above his eyebrow trickled down the side of his face, and he zeroed in on the entertained expression on Nasir's face.

"Now this is the show I've waited to see!" he exclaimed, clapping his hands. "The great Caesar King alone! Nobody to save him. How does it feel to know you're about to die? Finish him, James."

"You remember . . . how you said earlier that real power is patient?" Caesar said breathily with one eye swollen shut. James walked slowly to him, cracking his fists. "You said it's patient and always waiting for the right time to *strike!*"

The moment James was close enough, Caesar grabbed the gun from his waist and fired upward into his chin. Blood and brains exploded from the top of his head and came down on Caesar like rain. When James fell, he hit the ground so hard the floor shook. Nasir jumped backward when Caesar pointed the gun at him.

"The tranquilizer wore off a while ago. I was just waiting for the opportunity to make my move."

Nasir tried to get out of the way of the gun's sight, but Caesar followed his every move. All the anger that had lain dormant for so many years came flooding back to Caesar. Even though the outcome had been much more income, he would never forgive Nasir for killing Cassius. He was for sure going to kill him that time. There was no secret bookshelf he could fall into. But first, Caesar wanted him to suffer. He moved his aim from Nasir's forehead to his torso and fired the gun.

"Fuck!" Nasir shouted in pain as he fell back into the wall behind him. He clutched the side that the bullet had entered and tried to stay rooted on his feet. "You just shot me!"

"Shut up!" Caesar shot him again, that time in the leg.

Nasir dropped to the ground once the bullet inserted itself in his thigh. He shouted many more curses at Caesar, but the agony in his words was music to Caesar's ears. With a limp leg and a bleeding abdomen, Nasir leaned against the wall, helpless.

"Any last words?" Caesar asked and prepared to dim his light forever.

"Yes, actually," Nasir said and reached in his pocket and pulled out what looked like a small remote control. "Something told me to have a plan B. You were always a slimy son of a bitch, but I wasn't going to let you get away this time. No."

"What is that?" Caesar asked, and Nasir laughed through his labored breathing.

"I knew that after Namir's failed attempt to kill Boogie, he would lead me right to you. In preparation for that, I lined the entire building with explosives. Once I press this button, the bombs in each room will detonate exactly one minute apart from each other. I did it in such a way so that I would ensure my safe escape as well as my son's. But it's looking like none of us are going to be making it out."

"Noo!"

Caesar lunged for Nasir, but it was too late. Nasir pressed the button. Boom! The first explosive went off in the room across the hall and blew the door to that meeting room off its hinges. If Nasir told the truth, Caesar only had one minute until the next bomb went off. He couldn't waste any time. He had to find Boogie.

"Burn in hell!" he shouted and squeezed the trigger one more time.

The bullet pierced right between his eyes and exited through the back of his head. When he fell to the floor, blood poured from the wound and onto the dirty marble floor. Nasir's eyes were still open, frozen in the moment.

Dropping the gun, Caesar started to run but stumbled in pain to the ground. His body was aching and threatening to shut down on him, but he refused to let it no matter how much it hurt. He pushed through the pain and shakily stood back up. His run started up slowly, but he built up momentum with each step. He looked in each room he passed for Boogie, but there was no sign of him. There was another loud boom behind him and a minute later another one. The entire structure of the building would come crashing down any moment. Finally, when Caesar came out of the hallway and into what used to be the main floor of the museum, he spotted Boogie on the ground in front of Namir. A gun was pointed to his head, and Caesar had to act quickly.

Caesar ran and tackled him just as the bomb in there went off with another loud booming sound. He and Namir rolled on the ground, and the gun slid on the floor. The explosion made one of the main structural pillars fall, and part of the ceiling came crashing down. As they rolled, Caesar forcefully pushed Namir from on top of him just as another piece of the ceiling fell. The last thing Caesar saw of him was a look of pure hate before he was crushed.

"Boogie!" Caesar shouted and got to his feet. He could barely make out anything around him because of the debris and smoke from the fire. "Boogie!"

"I'm here!" he heard him call.

He stumbled in the direction of Boogie's voice and found him on the ground. He had his back against one of the pieces of the building that had fallen from the ceiling and had used it to cut the zip tie on his wrists.

"Let me help you," Caesar said, and together they snapped the zip ties on his ankles.

Seeing the state Caesar was in, Boogie hurried to his feet to help him. Caesar leaned on him, feeling his energy leaving him by the second. They made it to the front exit of the museum when another explosion went off. That one knocked them off their feet and separated them. Caesar got back to his feet coughing. When the debris cleared, he was able to see that the exit was blocked by a huge part of the ceiling. There was only a hole big enough for him to see through. Boogie was on the other side, clear to make it to safety.

"Caesar!" Boogie shouted when he realized what had happened. He rushed to the blockage and started throwing rubble to the side, trying with all his might to get him out. "Caesar!"

"Boogie, go!" Caesar told him, but his request was ignored. "Boogie, you have to go."

"I'm not leavin' you behind!" Boogie said and threw a big boulder to the side.

"Listen, son, you'll die if you stay here. This whole place is going to come crashing down at any second."

"No. No!" Boogie wasn't trying to hear him.

He just kept picking up rubble and trying to move it out of the way. It was heartbreaking for Caesar to watch. Tears flowed freely down his face, and he saw matching ones streaming down Boogie's.

"Boogie, it's hopeless. I'm not getting out of here," he was able to choke out. "Come here."

He put his arm through the hole and grabbed Boogie's forearm. Boogie did the same to him and tried to hold back his frustrated sob. His lips were trembling, and he stared into Caesar's beat-up face.

"I gotta get you out, man," he said. "I gotta try."

"Time is the thing we want most but the thing we use in the worst ways. There are so many things I wish I could have done differently. But I've lived a good life, Boogie," Caesar told him, feeling the warmth from his tears on his cheeks. "I'm okay with this. As long as you live. I've said it before, but I'm so proud of the man you've become. And I wish I could be around to see you become greater. But these are my cards, and I'm playing them how they were dealt. You will always be the son I never had. I love you."

"I love you too," Boogie got out.

There was one final explosion, and Caesar pushed Boogie away when the rest of the ceiling in the front came pummeling down on him. The only sound that could be heard was the wreckage piling up and Boogie's sorrowful shout of grief.

Precious Lord, take my hand
Lead me on, let me stand
I am tired, I am weak, I am worn

Boogie stood with Roz and held Amber in his arms at the burial site. Roz gripped his hand tightly and leaned onto his shoulder, sobbing softly. Boogie didn't care who saw the tears sliding down his face as the gospel song was being sung. Everyone standing around the casket at the burial site had tears streaming down their faces. They all shared the same pain and the same loss. Caesar King had touched all of their lives, and New York had lost its godfather.

Diana, the last of their predecessors alive, stood by Milli, Morgan, and Bentley. She wore a hat on her head with a veil that covered her face. She was trying to be strong for both Milli and Morgan, but it seemed as if they were all holding each other up. Brokenhearted was the only way to describe the mood of everyone in attendance.

The homegoing was very intimate with only family and Caesar's dearest loved ones. But even with only them, there were a lot of people. Zo stood beside Nathan and Nicky, comforting them. The thing they all had in common was that they shared the pain of losing a father figure twice. When Caesar's cousin Samantha stopped singing, she stepped aside and passed Nicky the mic. He stepped forward and wiped his eye before he started to speak.

"There's a lot that I could sit up here and say about Unc, but if he touched you in any way, you know the vibes," he said, sniffling. "He wasn't a perfect man, but he was loyal. And . . . and if I knew the last time I saw him was the last time I ever would again, I would have told him how much he meant to me. Milli, you know I got you through whatever, understand? It's for life with me."

"I know." Milli nodded.

Shortly after, she buried her head in Diana's neck and cried. Morgan patted her back as Diana rocked her. It was truly a sad day.

"I could go on for hours, but I have this lump in my throat that's not allowing me to continue. It's the weirdest thing." Nicky sniffled and wiped his eyes. He turned to Boogie and extended the mic. "Boogie, why don't you come and take over for me?"

All eyes went to Boogie as he slowly made his way to Nicky. After he took the mic and placed a hand on the golden casket, he took a deep, shaky breath and wiped his nose before he spoke.

"Caesar and I didn't get as much time together as probably the rest of you, but in the time we had, he helped me grow into the man my own father could be proud of. A part of me was hopin' that he would miraculously be alive again this time, but we didn't get so lucky." He had to stop because he got too choked up to continue.

"Take your time, baby!" somebody in the crowd said, and that gave him the strength he needed to continue.

"One of the things he said to me was that time is what we want the most but what we use the worst. But I have to disagree with him on this one. Caesar used his time more wisely than most. Somehow he managed to be a businessman, father, uncle, mentor, and friend. And not just sometimes. He did this every day. There will never be another man like Caesar King. So if I've learned anything from his life and teachings, it's to always be the best man I can be and live life to my fullest potential. I understand the lesson now. And for that I thank you."

Boogie kissed his hand and placed it back down on the casket. He stepped back and stood beside Nicky. Bentley made his way up to them and patted them both on the back. They were silent as they watched the gold casket begin to be lowered six feet into the ground. Boogie wiped his face, and when the casket was all the way in the ground, he tossed a white rose in, saying his final goodbye.

Nicky, Zo, Morgan, and Bentley followed suit. And when Boogie walked away so the rest of the family could speak their last words of peace, they went with him. He wanted to be alone, but then again, he didn't need to be. None of them did. They went to where all the cars were parked at the grave site and leaned against the hearse with long faces.

"So what's next now that Caesar is gone?" Morgan finally spoke.

"Unc would want us to continue business as usual. One man doesn't stop the show. I guess."

"He's right. We're bonded now. In money, in war, in loss, and in blood," Zo said.

"What about love?" Morgan asked.

"I would die for any one of you, so I guess that's love," Zo answered.

"Same," she said.

"Same," Nicky spoke.

"You already know what it is with me," Bentley said and took Morgan's hand.

They all looked to Boogie, who hadn't said anything yet. It dawned on him that although Nicky was the one who would take Caesar's place, it was Boogie they all looked to. All the power he once ran from had nestled comfortably in his lap. He nodded his head at their eager faces.

"The first thing we need to do is sit down and make a new pact. Mix some of the old with the new. Bentley?"

"What's good?"

"You showed me that it's not just on you, it's in you. I want you at the table, not as my right hand, but as a boss. I'm good with runnin' Brooklyn if you can handle the Island. Add some of your people to the fold."

"You already know I'ma hold it down." Bentley slapped Boogie's hand with his free one.

"Okay. Let's do this shit the hood way," Nicky said. He walked away to go to his car, and when he came back, he had a bottle of Hennessy and cups for them all. "Let's toast up to Unc."

When everybody had their shot, they put their cups in the air. Boogie was waiting for Nicky to say the toast, but once again everybody was looking at him. A small smile came to his face. He would have to get adjusted to being the go-to guy now that Caesar was gone.

"So much has been thrown at us individually and as a unit," he started and looked each of them in their eyes. "But the fact that we're still standing is a testament to our vigor. We'll always be stronger together because together everything is possible. And we have Caesar to thank for that. He'll never be forgotten because his legacy will live on through us. The five families of New York!"

Endings

Epilogue

"Such a nice homegoing," said the shaky voice belonging to an elderly white man who stood on a hill in the far distance.

He peered down and watched a small group of young people making a toast at a grave site. He had been there for the entire ceremony and had enjoyed the celebration of life. In his whole life he'd only heard of one other person being buried in a golden casket. And it just so happened that they were right next to each other. He hummed the tune of "Take My Hand Precious Lord" and stepped away from the hill to walk to the awaiting Rolls-Royce. A hand found its way to his elbow to assist him, and he snatched it away from his companion.

"Dammit! Stop trying to help me all the time before I have you arrested," he said, glaring at the tall black man.

"Jacob, you haven't been a detective for a long time. Plus, you work for me, remember?"

"Not anymore, I don't! You're dead. I just watched you get buried with my own eyes."

Caesar King laughed but then grimaced at the pain he felt in his healing ribs. He was trying to help his old friend when really it was he who needed some assistance down the hill. He had wanted so badly to go down and announce his presence, but he knew that, for a while, it was best he didn't. Still, that didn't make it any easier to watch everyone break down from the loss of him.

Back at the museum, Nasir had been right when he said that Caesar knew the place like the back of his hand. When the ceiling at the exit came crashing down, it looked to Boogie that he had been crushed by it. But he hadn't been. Caesar used what little oxygen he had left to locate the crawl space Paul had shown him years ago. He barely had made it out when the entire building came crashing down. From behind the building he could hear Boogie's screams, and the hardest thing Caesar had ever done in his life was walk away like he hadn't.

Caesar somehow managed to get to his old friend Jacob Easley's home and get patched up. Jacob called in one final favor, and that favor was the body they had in the golden casket. After

Caesar killed Nasir, he realized that he'd put the last of his demons to bed. He was ready to move on to the next chapter of his life. But he knew that if any of his loved ones knew of his survival, he would always be tempted to go back. So he chose to let them believe he was dead. He had money in offshore accounts and a private jet nobody knew about. He would be just fine.

"You know you can't tell Michael about this, right?" Caesar asked, helping Jacob into the car.

"I won't. And hell, I only have about six months to live anyways. Your secret will die with me."

Caesar shut Jacob's door and went over to the driver's side. When he got in, he sighed and said goodbye to his old life. He drove away without looking into the rearview mirror once. Jacob was dying of cancer, and it was true that the doctors had given him six months to live. Caesar couldn't think of a better way to repay him for all his years of service than to send him home with a bang.

"So where do you want to spend the next six months of your life?"

"On a beach with beautiful women. Lots of beautiful women."

"I think I know just the place," Caesar told him.

"Good." Jacob leaned back in his seat and got as comfortable as he could. "You think you'll ever come back here?"

"I've come back from the dead before, so who knows? Maybe." Caesar's lips spread into a slow smile as the sun beamed on his face. "Maybe."